THE
ALABASTER
JAR

VOLUME 2: ANCIENT ELEMENTS

MARIE SONTAG

SUNBURY
P R E S S
Mechanicsburg, PA USA

Published by Sunbury Press, Inc.
50 West Main Street
Mechanicsburg, Pennsylvania 17055

www.sunburypress.com

Copyright © 2015 by Marie Sontag.
Cover Copyright © 2015 by Daniel Sontag.

For information about special discounts for bulk purchases, please contact Sunbury Press Orders Dept. at (855) 338-8359 or orders@sunburypress.com.

To request one of our authors for speaking engagements or book signings, please contact Sunbury Press Publicity Dept. at publicity@sunburypress.com.

ISBN: 978-1-62006-621-8 (Trade Paperback)
ISBN: 978-1-62006-622-5 (Mobipocket)

Library of Congress Control Number: 2015950831

FIRST SUNBURY PRESS EDITION: September 2015

Product of the United States of America
0 1 1 2 3 5 8 13 21 34 55

Set in Bookman Old Style
Designed by Crystal Devine
Cover by Daniel Sontag
Cover photo © mihtiander/123RF.com
Illustrations by Marsha Owen
Edited by Celeste Helman

Continue the Enlightenment!

Dedication

The Alabaster Jar is dedicated to Jon and Rachel whose intertwined souls have worked long and hard to sculpt their own alabaster jar from the elements of their combined talents and passions. It is also dedicated to the memory of my 6th grade social studies teacher, Adele Minnie, who stirred within me a love for ancient civilizations.

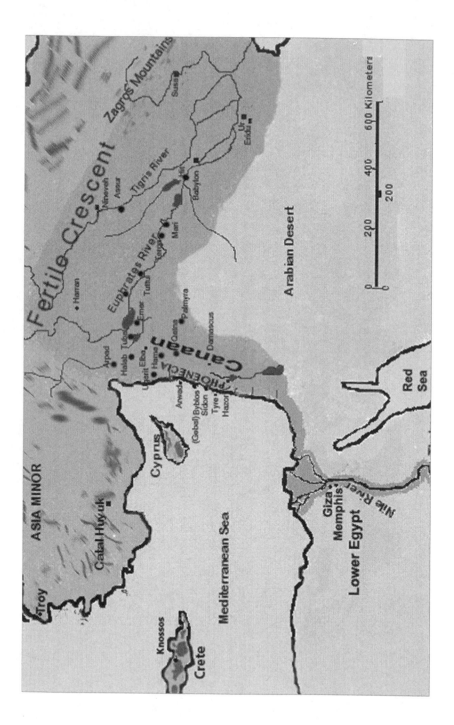

ONE

Memphis, Egypt—Peret (Season of Planting) 1778 BC

When fourteen-year-old Samsuluna saw the scrawny scribe grab the priest's robed arm, Sam stepped back into the shadow of a limestone column.

"We just uncovered the entrance to an undiscovered tomb near Giza," the administrative scribe told Nakthor, the lector priest.

Sam saw Nakthor cup his hand on the side of his mouth. "Does anyone know about this yet?"

The short scribe shook his baldhead. "Only our two workers."

Even in the dim light of Memphis' setting sun, Sam saw Nakthor's bottom lip curl into a half-smile. "Draw me a map and start our usual process tomorrow." Nakthor then gripped the scribe's shoulder. "But make sure no one sees you. This must remain a secret."

Sam stepped further into the column's shadow and waited for the two men to leave the compound of the House of Scrolls. He never liked Nakthor. Every morning Sam endured Nakthor's high-pitched voice as the priest recited prayers and incantations for the day. And whenever Sam and his adoptive father, Balashi, left with the Egyptian Chief Physician to visit patients in the city of Memphis, they first had to get permission from the priest. Nakthor always granted it, but he never failed to make condescending remarks about Sam and Balashi's Babylonian citizenship. More than once, Sam heard Nakthor refer to them as unwelcomed foreigners.

Sam shook his head and wondered what he should do about Nakthor's cryptic conversation. He absent-mindedly touched his tunic where he kept his bronze dagger hidden. Since his near-death experience with the caravan driver in Babylonia two years ago, Sam made sure the dagger never left his side.

As Sam limped home to join his adoptive sister, Amata, for their evening meal, he chewed his lower lip. With each step, he thrust his walking stick deeper into the soft ground as if to tamp down his worried thoughts. Balashi should be going home with him.

Two years had passed since Balashi, the great Babylonian physician, adopted him. At first, Amata seemed unwilling to share her father with Sam, having lost her mother at the age of six to an illness even Balashi couldn't cure. Gradually, however, the trio grew into a tight-knit family—until their recent move to Egypt.

Sam realized that, lately, Balashi only tore himself away from his study of Egyptian papyri at the House of Scrolls for an occasional visit with a patient. At least, since Sam was still in training, he always accompanied Balashi. In the evening, however, Balashi usually didn't come home from his studies until long after Sam and Amata went to bed. The more time Balashi spent away from home, the more Amata appeared depressed and distant. Lately she spent much of her free time with the Egyptian princesses at their winter residence in Memphis. Sam feared that Amata was beginning to adopt many Egyptian ways at the expense of her Babylonian identity. He couldn't even count how many scarab amulets she recently purchased. More importantly, he worried that Balashi's constant absence would make Amata feel more like he once felt—an orphan. Sam realized his worst fears when he walked into the main room of their Egyptian mud-brick house.

Amata's normally long black hair barely covered her ears.

Sam gasped. "What did you do to your hair?" He ran over to where Amata sat on her cushion by the eating table. Sam tugged on a strand, as if to make it longer.

2

Amata jerked her head away from Sam. "I visited with Princess Miut today and she suggested I cut my hair in the Egyptian style. That way it's easier to wear the new, fashionable wigs."

Sam stared at Amata for a moment and then sat on his cushion on the other side of the low table. He had no idea fourteen-year-old girls could be so exasperating. "So Princess Miut cut your hair?" Sam wrinkled his nose.

Amata frowned. "No, silly. Her hairdresser cut my hair."

Just then their Egyptian cook, Eshe, carried in a brass platter filled with emmer wheat flatbread, and placed it between Sam and Amata.

"*Dua Netjer en et.* Thank you." Amata nodded and smiled at the cook.

Eshe gave a slight bow and returned to the cooking area in the front courtyard.

Sam watched their Egyptian cook leave and then faced Amata. "Practicing your Egyptian, I see."

Amata raised her chin. "I spend my whole day with Egyptians, so why shouldn't I speak their language whenever I can?" Amata picked up a piece of flatbread and spread it with *fūl* made from beans and spices. She took a bite and chewed it slowly, watching Sam.

Amata, like their tawny, yellow-gray cat, Bastet, sat very still but looked ready to pounce. Sam tried to think of a way to defuse the conversation. "I've been thinking about Balashi and me being away so much." Sam paused to pick up a piece of flatbread. "I know you spend your mornings at home with tutors to learn more of the Egyptian language and culture, and most of your afternoons with the princesses at the winter residence." Sam bit off a corner of the coarse bread and chewed, the scent of garlic and onion tickling his nose. "But why don't we take a trip tomorrow to the pyramids at Giza?"

Amata stared at the plate of bread that sat between them. "I would love that, Sam. It's been a long time since we've all done something together. Father spends so much time studying; I think he's even forgotten my name."

Sam cleared his throat. "Well, I meant just the two of us. I think Father has several important appointments with patients tomorrow."

"Oh. Of course he does. How silly of me." Amata's voice sounded tight. "Just the two of us then."

"So, it's all settled." Sam slapped his leg and tried to sound cheerful. "Tomorrow morning we'll go down to the Delta first, then on to Giza." Sam picked up the last piece of bread and took a bite. Talking around the chunks, he added, "I want to introduce you to a friend of mine. He works in a sculptor's workshop on the Delta. He's actually a Canaanite slave of the Master Sculptor, but mid-morning his master gives him some free time, so we can visit him then."

Amata's eyebrows rose. "How did you meet this Canaanite slave?"

"Balashi and I stitched up his finger when he cut it a few weeks ago. His name is Keret." Sam took a sip of his barley drink and then continued. "Keret's got a great sense of humor, and yet he's quite the gentleman. He gave Balashi a gift for stitching his finger, even though his master, Fenuku, paid for our services. Keret's two years older than we are, but he reminds me a lot of Enlil."

Sam saw the corners of Amata's eyes pinch together. He guessed she missed their Babylonian friend as much as he did.

Amata finished her bread then sat up on her knees. "Well, I agree to visit Keret as long as you promise that we'll see the Giza pyramids. They're very sacred, you know."

Sam rubbed his chin. "It's about 320 rods from Memphis to Giza, but maybe the Master Sculptor will loan us his donkey. Think you can handle a two-hour donkey ride there and back?"

Amata smiled. "Are you measuring the distance by Babylonian rods or Egyptian rods?"

Sam shrugged his shoulders. "There's a difference?"

Amata just rolled her eyes.

Sam laughed, happy to see the color return to Amata's face once again.

After their evening meal, Amata and Sam walked outside. From their mud-brick house they could see the Nile in the distance. Light from the full moon shimmered off the river. Sam wondered if he should tell Amata about the conversation he heard between Nakthor and the scribe.

4

His adventurous spirit finally got the best of him and he related the enigmatic exchange.

"So, when we visit the Giza pyramids tomorrow," he concluded, "maybe we could poke around for that hidden tomb."

Amata frowned. "As long as you don't get us into trouble. I still haven't recovered from all the excitement your curiosity caused us in Babylon."

The next morning, having received Balashi's permission, Sam and Amata walked the short distance to the mouth of the Delta. The port at Peru-Nefer harbored not only ships, but also a dense array of workshops, factories and warehouses that distributed food and merchandise throughout the kingdom.

Sam found Keret behind the Master Sculptor's workshop eating a quick snack of dried fish. "Amata, I'd like you to meet my friend Keret," Sam said. "Keret, this is my sister, Amata."

Keret tossed his now empty fish bones into the river and then wiped his hands on the kilt skirt around his waist. "You said she was pretty, but you were wrong."

Amata stepped back. Sam saw her eyes grow large. If Keret was trying to charm his sister, it wasn't working.

"She's not pretty," Keret said and then laughed. "She's beautiful!"

Sam pushed Keret's shoulder and laughed along with him.

Amata blushed. She fingered one of the long beaded braids in her new black wig. "And I thought you said Keret was a gentleman," Amata shot back.

"Maybe not a gentleman." Sam smiled. "But he's a great sculptor." Sam glanced toward the workshop. "Why don't you show Amata some of your work."

Sam and Amata followed Keret into the workshop. Sam rubbed his nose as he breathed in the dusty, sharp smell of hammered stone mixed with the vinegar-like odor of men's sweat. Sam caught Amata eying Keret's bare copper chest that rippled with muscles as Keret moved a heavy piece of limestone to the end of his wooden work table and placed a small piece of calcite in its place.

"The Master Sculptor gave me this piece of calcite because it has a slight flaw." Sam saw that Keret was carving an alabaster jar out of the piece of calcite. Sam had learned about different kinds of minerals, like calcite, when he and Balashi studied in the House of Scrolls. Sam found it fascinating that medicines could be extracted from certain kinds of rocks.

Sam fingered the stone. "Calcite's found in limestone, right?"

Keret nodded. "How did you know that?"

"I read that Egyptian physicians use calcite to make a white powder to treat certain stomach pains, and that we can find calcite in limestone."

Keret pointed to a spot where the alabaster jar had a thin crack. "Here's where the calcite is flawed, but I knew I could still make something beautiful out of it. When I'm finished," he lowered his voice, "I want to give the jar to Princess Miut as a present."

Amata touched the unfinished rim of the jar. "Princess Miut could use a new alabaster jar. She has more makeup and perfumes than she has containers to put them in."

Keret looked up. "Have you met her?"

"Yes." Amata nodded. "I visit their Memphis palace almost every afternoon."

Keret picked up the small jar with his large hand. "Good. Then maybe you can give this to Princess Miut when I'm done."

Amata smiled. "I would be delighted. I think she'll love it. I know I would."

Just then a broad, bare-chested Egyptian wearing a white linen cloth around his waist entered the workshop. "Keret," the large man said in a deep voice. "It's time to get back to work."

Keret looked again at Amata. "Come back in two weeks and I'll have this finished."

"Then I'll see you in two weeks." Amata fingered one of her braids again and lowered her eyes.

TWO

The three great pyramids at Giza loomed large overhead. Sam craned his neck to see the top of Khufu's pyramid. He wondered if it was higher than their revered ziggurat in Babylon.

Amata seemed to read Sam's mind. "Khufu's pyramid is about one-third higher than our Babylonian temple, *Et-em-en-an-ki*," Amata said.

Sam let out a low whistle. "Amazing." Sam moved closer and touched one of the large limestone blocks at the base of Khufu's pyramid. In his other hand he tightly gripped the papyrus-fibered rope that tethered the donkey to him. The Master Sculptor had loaned them his donkey for the day, and Sam wanted to make sure he returned it in good condition. "I wonder how old these pyramids are." Sam shook his head in awe.

Amata joined Sam at the base of the pyramid. "The Egyptians don't keep track of time the way we do. For them, history goes in circles, not in a straight line."

Sam's forehead creased. "Huh?"

Amata laughed. "When my tutor explained it to me for the first time, I didn't get it either." Amata sat in the shade provided by the donkey and leaned back against the pyramid.

Sam lifted the edge of a heavy stone and secured the donkey's lead rope beneath it. He then pulled a handful of dried dates out of the leather pouch slung across the donkey's back and joined Amata in the small strip of shade. When he sat down, he noticed Amata tracing circles in the sand with her finger.

Amata must have noticed his puzzled look. "I'm trying to think of a way to explain Egyptian time." Amata pursed her lips and looked out over the sand. "The Egyptians don't pass down stories to their children about their heroes the way we do. Take for example, our Babylonian legend of Gilgamesh. His epic story teaches us that he was the fifth king of the city-state of Uruk. From what my Egyptian tutor tells me about lists of Egyptian kings, Gilgamesh probably ruled in Sumer around the same time that Khufu built this pyramid."

"What does that have to do with time going in circles or a straight line?" Sam scratched his head.

Amata smirked. "I'm getting to that. The Egyptians have myths about what their gods and goddesses did in the past, but they don't hand down stories about people from the past, like our hero, Gilgamesh. For them, the past isn't something to learn from or copy in the present." Amata sighed. "In a way, it's like the past is never past. For example, Ra carries the sun across the sky every day, through the underworld at night, and then reappears with it again in the morning. As long as the pharaohs keep society stable, things continue the way they've always been. Ra continues to journey across the sky and we continue to have day and night, season after season. That's what's important to them—more important than keeping records about what ruler reigned during a certain time period."

"Well now, that really clears things up." Sam shook his head in confusion.

Sam and Amata sat in silence for a few moments. Sam watched a scarab beetle roll a ball of dung to a spot near a corner of a pyramid stone. The beetle then dug a hole and dropped the dung ball in it. Sam excitedly tugged on Amata's arm and pointed to the bug. "I just saw a scarab beetle lay an egg on top of its dung ball and then bury it."

"Eeew." Amata scrunched up her nose. "That's disgusting."

Sam's lower lip protruded. "It's not disgusting. I think it's fascinating." Sam recalled asking Balashi why so many Egyptians wore scarab seals and amulets. Balashi had explained that, to the Egyptians, the scarab symbolized rebirth or regeneration. "When a scarab buries a ball of dung," Balashi said, "it deposits an egg on it, and then buries it as part of its reproductive cycle. When its egg hatches, the grub feeds on the ball of dung under the ground until it turns into a beetle. Later, the new beetle emerges from the ground and repeats the cycle." *Why couldn't Amata understand how fascinating that was?*

Amata looked over at Sam. "Oh, don't pout." She laughed. "I like history and culture. You like science and medicine. It's okay to get excited about different things." Suddenly Amata grabbed Sam's arm. "That's it, Sam!"

Sam cocked his head to the side. "That's what?"

"That's how to explain the different way Egyptians view time. You and I see life differently. You look at life through the eyes of science, trying to understand how things work. I mostly ask "why" questions, especially about history and culture. In a similar way, Egyptians and Babylonians see life differently, especially time. Egyptians look at life by seeing how cycles repeat themselves. Babylonians see life as constantly moving forward and revealing new things."

Sam finished his last date. "That sort of makes sense."

Amata leaned forward and drew again in the sand. "For Egyptians, life is like a circle. To us, life is like a straight line. The story of Ra ferrying the sun across the sky every day, going into the underworld, and then coming up again the next day is important because it's a picture of the cycle of life. That's why Egyptians revere the scarab beetle as sacred. It symbolizes this idea of life as a circle, death and rebirth. It also explains why keeping things the same is important to Egyptians. For them, if things stay the same, patterns can continue to repeat themselves. But for us, we've been taught that life is something that constantly moves forward, revealing new things to learn and better ways to do things, like you and Father wanting to find better ways to heal people." Amata scrunched up her nose.

"Well, it made more sense in my head before I said it out loud."

Suddenly Sam's eyes widened.

Amata smiled. "So you understand what I mean?"

Sam pointed off to the right. "No, but I think I just saw someone come out of that sand dune over there."

Amata's gaze followed his finger. "That's silly. You can't come out of a sand dune." She leaned her head forward and squinted. "Oh wait. I think I do see something."

A small figure moved along a sand dune off in the distance and then disappeared behind it. Then another small image emerged, as if from within the dune. It looked like the second person carried something heavy.

Sam almost whispered. "We should take a closer look."

Amata's eyes narrowed. "Sam, are you going to get us into something dangerous?"

"Who me?" Sam flashed a smile. "Come on, I know you love adventure *almost* as much as I do." Sam stood and offered Amata his hand.

His adoptive sister brushed the sand off her long white linen dress and grabbed Sam's hand. "I know I'm going to regret this, but let's go."

When they reached the sand dune, they found it abandoned. A few granite boulders dotted the area. Sam secured the donkey's rope under one of them. He and Amata explored the area, but couldn't find an opening.

"Over here," Sam finally called out. Sam grunted as he tried to push a boulder away from a sand-covered hill. Then, using his walking stick for leverage, he managed to nudge the large rock forward, revealing an entrance.

Amata peered inside. "If we go in, we won't be able to see a thing. It'll be totally dark."

Sam rubbed his jaw. "I hadn't thought about that. Why don't you stay out here with Fenuku's donkey. I'll go in and just feel my way around. I won't be long."

Sam saw Amata glance at his crippled leg. "But what if you fall?" Amata hesitated.

Before she could say any more, Sam ducked and limped inside.

Ten minutes later, Sam came out. "I went down a narrow entryway that opened up into what seemed like a small room," he told Amata. "I felt several large clay jars with lids. The lids had some kind of seal on them. Although I couldn't see anything, the seal felt like it might have been in the shape of a scarab beetle."

Amata clapped her hands. "Oh, Sam! That could be the seal of some previous Egyptian king. I could ask my tutor if he knows what pharaoh might have used that seal. The next time we come, let's bring a hot coal and an oil lamp for light so we can explore some more."

Sam grinned. "Next, time, huh?"

THREE

For the next two weeks, Balashi kept Sam busy visiting patients, learning new treatments, and studying in the House of Scrolls. Sam had no free time to investigate the tomb, but that didn't prevent him from thinking about it. He kept a close eye on Nakthor and his assistant, but heard nothing more about the hidden tomb.

Today Balashi assigned Sam to study papyri penned by embalming physicians and instructed him to look for information relating to the lungs. Sam knew that Balashi suspected an illness related to the lungs had caused the death of Amata's mother. And since the mummification process gave Egyptian physicians the opportunity to study the human body in greater detail than healers in other countries where embalming wasn't practiced, Sam worked hard to focus his thoughts. If Sam could help Balashi find out what caused Amata's mother's death, perhaps Balashi would find some peace. With each passing day, Balashi grew more obsessed with finding out what caused his wife's death. Sometimes Balashi worked all day and never stopped to eat. "If I can find the cause, then perhaps I can find the cure," Balashi told Sam on more than one occasion.

Although finding out what caused Amata's mother's death wouldn't bring her back, Sam hoped that it would at least return Sam's family life back to the way it was before they left Babylon. For the first time in his life, Sam felt like he belonged. He feared that the growing tension between Balashi and Amata would take that away. When Balashi saw Amata's short hair, he forbade her to visit the princesses ever again. Balashi and Amata stopped talking to each other for a week. Amata finally apologized and agreed to ask Balashi's permission before she changed her appearance or visited the palace, so Balashi had relented. And yet, Sam still saw evidence of their frayed relationship in the short, clipped way Amata spoke to her father, or in how Balashi often left in the morning without saying goodbye to her.

Sam tried to push away thoughts about his family and focus on the scroll in front of him. It described how embalmers removed the body's brain by inserting a metal rod up the nose and then breaking through to the braincase. Suddenly, Qar, the Chief Physician, interrupted him.

"We have been summoned to see the Master Sculptor," Qar told Sam and Balashi.

Sam looked up into the lined face of the Chief Physician. Crinkles of worry appeared on Qar's forehead. As was his habit, the elderly physician tucked a loose strand of gray hair underneath his black wig.

Before Qar could give any more details, the lector priest, Nakthor, approached their table. The priest's colorful robe billowed around him. Nakthor narrowed his eyes at Sam and Balashi and then turned to address Qar.

"I will allow the foreigners to accompany you to see the Master Sculptor," Nakthor said, "but only because his recovery is of the utmost importance. The Master Sculptor has several unfinished statues he must complete for Pharaoh's tomb and for the temple of Ptah. Because of the severity of his illness, I will also accompany you so that I can recite the sacred texts."

Qar opened his mouth but quickly closed it again. Sam guessed that the physician knew better than to argue with Nakthor. He knew that the Chief Physician, like Balashi, believed in finding natural cures for patients. Unlike most healers, Qar had limited faith in magic or sacred texts.

———— • ————

When Sam and the three adults reached the sculptor's home, Keret greeted them at the door and led them into his master's chamber.

The Chief Physician immediately went to the sculptor's bedside. "Fenuku, my old friend. Why didn't you call for us sooner?"

Fenuku inhaled short breaths through his mouth. "It's nothing," he gasped. "I just need to rest for a few days."

Qar gently laid his palm on Fenuku's head. "Do you have pain?"

"My chest hurts when I breathe."

Keret interjected. "He's had chest pain and trouble breathing all season. This past week he's developed a cough and a fever."

Balashi stepped forward. "Has he coughed up blood?"

Keret's lips pinched together. "Yes. He started spitting up blood yesterday."

Nakthor pushed the two physicians aside. Sam saw small beads of perspiration form on Nakthor's bony bald head. "We must first cleanse his entire body, invoke the powers of Heka, and then offer up prayers and incantations to Sekhmet, the god of healing. The foreigners must leave the room immediately. They are not permitted to hear the sacred words."

"Keret," the Chief Physician lowered his voice. "Have the servants draw warm water with which to wash Fenuku, but bring a cold compress for his forehead."

Keret bowed and then left the room with Sam and Balashi.

Sam and Balashi helped the servants prepare the water and then went outside to wait for the priest to recite his sacred texts. Sam shielded his eyes from the late afternoon sun and took in the view of the other whitewashed mud-brick homes in the craftsmen's area of the city. Although the Master Sculptor oversaw work for Pharaoh's palace, the tomb complex, and the temple of Ptah, Fenuku's home looked no larger than the other squarish living quarters in the area.

After a few minutes, Balashi finally spoke. "I've seen these symptoms before. I'm afraid Fenuku may be suffering from the same illness as Amata's late mother."

Sam took in a deep breath. "And we still don't know the cure, do we?"

Balashi shook his head. "I'm no closer to a cure than I was before I left Babylon."

Sam looked up and winced as he noticed dark circles beneath Balashi's eyes. "What about the Egyptian's channel theory you've told me about?" Sam tried to sound hopeful. "Could that give us a clue?"

A smile appeared on Balashi's face that didn't quite reach his eyes. "It's possible, Samsuluna. As I've always said, I do believe you have a gift for the healing arts."

Sam's words tumbled out. "I think it's possible that the channel theory could explain many things we don't understand. Just like how the Egyptian farmers have to constantly clean out the irrigation ditches that bring water from the Nile to their fields, it makes sense that many illnesses might be caused by the body's blocked channels."

"Yes." Balashi nodded. "I must agree. This is one of the most intriguing ideas I've learned yet from the Egyptians. No one in Babylon ever talks about the body having channels."

Sam continued. "When we were studying the embalmers' papyri this morning, before I read about how they take the brains out of the bodies they mummify, I read a papyrus about the lungs. It said embalmers discovered that the lungs and the spleen are connected to four vessels, which like the liver, are supplied with liquid and air. Since the Master Sculptor has trouble breathing, perhaps something in the channels to the lungs is blocking his air."

Balashi stroked his peppered beard that now contained more gray than black. "But exactly what are those channels, and how do we unblock them? Those are the questions I cannot answer."

"Then we'll just have to keep looking."

Suddenly the winds picked up, swirling dust and sand into circular pillars. Sam covered his mouth and nose with the sleeve of his tunic.

"Perhaps we should go back inside," Balashi said.

Once they rejoined Keret inside the house, Keret called over their cook.

"Anut," Keret said, "please bring us barley drinks and a plate of flatbread."

Anut nodded and quickly returned with the food and drinks. Sam saw that, even though Keret was Fenuku's slave, the household servants almost treated Keret as if he were Fenuku's son.

Keret, Balashi and Sam sat on mats around a low table and discussed Fenuku's illness and their hopes for his recovery.

"The priest doesn't seem at all concerned with Fenuku's well-being," Keret said in a low voice. "All he cares about is the completion of Pharaoh's statues."

Balashi took a piece of bread from the platter and then looked up at Keret. "You care for your master very much, don't you son?"

Keret nodded. "He's more of a father to me than a master. He bought me from Amorite traders when I was eight, and I have served him ever since. When I turn eighteen, he's promised to grant my freedom."

Sam cocked his head to the side. "Did Fenuku ever marry?"

"Not that I know of," Keret said. "Perhaps he's been too busy with his craft as a sculptor."

Keret left the room and returned with a small alabaster jar in hand. "Please give this to Amata," Keret told Sam. "Remember, she promised to give it to Princess Miut. Have her tell the princess that it's from a secret admirer."

Balashi raised an eyebrow. "Are you fond of Princess Miut?"

Keret's face grew red. "I know I'm just a slave and she's a princess," he admitted. "But when she and her mother come to our workshop to discuss statues for the winter palace, she always smiles at me. I think she likes me." Keret took a long sip from his cup.

Sam nodded. "And, after all, Princess Miut is the daughter of Pharaoh's second wife, not his first, so she's not really in line to become queen, right?"

Balashi cleared his throat. "It doesn't matter if Princess Miut is the daughter of Pharaoh's second, third, fourth, or fifth wife. It's my understanding that she's not allowed to marry below her status, even if Keret was a freeman. Also, unless special permission is granted, she's not allowed to marry a foreigner. I'm sorry Keret, but she's merely flirting with you. Do not take it to heart."

Keret handed the alabaster jar to Sam. "Well, things could change. Besides, Merib, the son of Pharaoh's first wife, doesn't seem very interested in Princess Miut, and there are no other royal men available. Maybe if I suddenly became rich, things would be different."

Sam took the jar from Keret. "Well, you can always dream."

Keret looked up at the palm-raftered ceiling and then at Sam. "Why didn't Amata come with you today? She said she'd come back in two weeks to pick up the alabaster jar."

Balashi stroked his beard. "Amata doesn't accompany us on physician calls."

"And besides," Sam interjected, "she went on a boat trip up the Nile with Princess Miut and her sisters for two weeks. Amata said that when Pharaoh visits with his administrators in the winter palace here in Memphis, the mothers take the children on excursions. Amata just left us a note to say she was going. She didn't even ask Balashi for permission."

Balashi cleared his throat. "No need to share our family business, Samsuluna." Sam looked up and saw Balashi's eyes narrow and his face darken.

Keret leaned forward. "Well, if Pharaoh is meeting with his administrators here, I hope he will exercise some control over the nomarch of the Memphis nome. This month the nomarch had his managers cut back the peoples' ration of grain and barley drink to minimal amounts. I know we've had inadequate rainfall, but I've heard that people in other nomes get larger amounts of necessities than we do. If you ask me, I think the nomarch or his managers are secretly selling off some of the surplus."

Keret cut his conversation short when Nakthor suddenly emerged from Fenuku's chamber. Nakthor spotted the alabaster jar in Sam's hand and pointed to it. "Was that made by the Master Sculptor?" the priest asked in his high-pitched voice.

Keret rose from his mat. His tall frame towered above the priest's bulbous head. "No, I made it."

The priest smiled and held out his hand to Sam. "Good. I will take it then."

Sam looked over at Balashi who slowly nodded. Sam handed the jar to Nakthor.

The priest smiled, revealing his yellowed teeth. "I've been looking for an appropriate gift for the royal household when I call on them at the winter palace this evening. You may join the Chief Physician in the sculptor's room now."

With that, Nakthor turned and left. Sam clenched his fists. He really hated people who abused their power.

FOUR

Amata looked forward to spending two weeks with Princess Miut and her sisters, sailing south up the Nile to visit their palace at Thebes. She felt a twinge of guilt for not having asked her father's permission, but his previous weeks of silence had left a sting that assuaged her guilt. She started to feel as though the royal family had adopted her as one of their own.

"I can't wait to show you my beautiful gowns," Princess Miut told Amata. The girls sat under the shade of the royal ship's canopy while servants fanned them with ostrich feathers. Four of Princess Miut's younger half-sisters sat with them.

Amata looked up to watch the boat's rectangular-shaped sail billow in the wind. Glare from the afternoon sun reflected off the Nile, and Amata lifted her hand to shield her eyes.

Princess Miut forced Amata's arm down. "Just hold still so I can apply the eyeliner. Once I'm finished, the sun's rays won't seem so strong." Miut held aloft a small white ivory stick and waited for the boat's rocking to stop. When it calmed, the princess leaned forward, dipped the stick into the black antimony-soot paste, and outlined Amata's eyes.

"There," the princess proudly announced.

Amata blinked, then waved away the flies from the copper plate of fruit that one of the servants placed in front of her. Amata picked up a small piece of watermelon and popped it into her mouth.

Princess Miut smiled. "The kohl eyeliner will also help keep the flies away. And, when you're done feasting, we'll apply the *udju*."

Amata didn't know what *udju* was, but she wasn't about to ask. She sat back in her wicker chair and closed her eyes. She enjoyed letting the refreshing watermelon juice remain in her mouth a moment longer. A cool river breeze brushed her face. She could get used to living the life of a royal, but she almost felt guilty. Her father and Sam worked hard every day trying to learn as much as possible about Egyptian medicine. She wished they would take a little more time off. At least Princess Miut valued her friendship enough to spend time with her.

"Okay my sister, *Princess* Amata," Miut teased. "Time for the green malachite eyeshadow."

Eye shadow. So that's what *udju* was. Since Sam was her only sibling, and an adopted one at that, Amata relished the thought that sixteen-year-old Princess Miut pretended to be her older sister.

Princess Miut stood and handed Amata a polished copper mirror. "Before we apply the *udju*, you might want to see your *wadjet* eyes first."

At least Amata understood the word *wadjet*. Amata took the mirror and stared at the black kohl outlining her dark-brown eyes. The lined patterns looked exactly like pictures she'd seen of the Eye of Horus.

"*Wadjet*, symbol of Horus, falcon god of the sky," Amata said aloud.

Princess Miut took back the mirror. "Yes, Horus. The falcon god who sees all. You know that Horus' right eye represents the sun, and his left eye represents the moon, don't you?"

Amata nodded. "Yes. Seth tore out Horus' left eye and broke it into pieces. But Thoth, with the help of the other gods, restored Horus' left eye by spitting on it."

Princess Miut smiled. "Correct. That is why we call Horus' left eye *wadjet*, meaning whole, or healthy, since Seth tore out Horus' left eye, and Thoth then restored it. The story of Horus' left eye, broken into pieces, is acted out in our world every month as we watch the moon disappear from the night sky and then slowly return. As royals, we put the *wadjet* on both eyes, not just the left, because we need more protection than most people. The symbol of Horus gives us that protection." Miut paused to place a hand on her hip and strike a pose. "And besides, it makes our makeup look more balanced to have the *wadjet* on both eyes, don't you think?"

"I suppose." Amata's eyebrows squeezed together. She wasn't ready yet to leave their discussion about Egyptian gods. "If Horus' left eye represents the changing phases of the moon, broken and then whole again, and his right eye represents the sun, why is Horus' right eye sometimes called the eye of Ra? And why is Ra, like Horus, also depicted as a falcon god? Are Ra and Horus the same god?"

Princess Miut waved a dismissive hand. "Girls shouldn't think so much. Besides, it's difficult to explain our beliefs to a foreigner."

Miut's remark stung, but she tried to make light of it. Amata gave Miut a mock frown. "I thought I was your sister, *Princess Amata*."

Princess Miut, still standing, reached down and patted Amata's arm. "And so you are. All right. I will try to explain." Miut sat next to Amata and ordered the slaves behind them to fan more vigorously.

"As Egyptians, we understand that our gods represent layers of reality. They help us explain and connect the world we can see with the world we can't see. Ra is often pictured as a falcon-man with the sun disk on his head. You'll also see Horus as a falcon god with the symbols of both Upper and Lower Egypt on his head. These images remind us that, like a falcon flying across the sky, all the gods watch over us and bring order to our lives, just as do the sun and the moon."

Miut's mother, sitting with them under the boat's canopy, broke into the conversation. "You see my dear Amata, we believe in two eternities. One is the eternity we can see, *neheh*. This is cyclical time that, like the scarab, continually renews itself. The other *djet* is the sacred dimension of everness where that which has ripened to its final form is preserved in unchangeable permanence."

Amata cocked her head to the side. "So the great stone tombs and the mummification of bodies are symbols of the eternity we can see moving into the sacred dimension we cannot see?"

Miut's mother nodded. "And Pharaoh, as the embodiment of Ra on earth, must maintain the stability of society so that the cycle of life continues uninterrupted. Our people understand that when there is disorder, chaos rules and the people suffer, upsetting both eternities."

Princess Miut rubbed her temples. "Enough philosophy, Mother. It makes my head hurt."

The princess turned to Amata. "Lean towards me Amata so that I can apply your eye shadow now."

Amata complied.

The princess removed the knobbed lid from a small alabaster jar and inserted an ivory stick into it. She stirred the green powder and then applied it above Amata's right eye.

Suddenly the boat jolted and an elderly servant bumped into the princess, knocking the alabaster jar out of her hand. The jar crashed to the deck and broke into several pieces. Green malachite powder sprinkled not only the deck, but also Miut's new slippers.

Princess Miut jumped up. "You stupid slave!" She shoved the bony, elderly man as he tried to rise up from where he'd fallen. He lost his balance again, tumbled backwards, and splashed into the water.

Amata, aghast at Miut's fury, stood and peered over the side. "Someone should help him!" Amata watched as the servant thrashed about, bobbing up and down. She doubted he could swim.

Miut shrugged. "I offer him up to Sobek. As Lord of the Waters and Protector of Pharaohs, Sobek was probably protecting me from some future evil by throwing this old slave into the waters."

Amata glanced at Princess Miut's mother. Pharaoh's second wife simply nodded her head in agreement, as did

22

Pharaoh's first wife, the mother of Prince Merib. No one moved to help the servant. Should she try to rescue the poor man? What would Miut and the pharaoh's wives think? No, she'd seen crocodiles swimming in these waters.

The boat sailed on, and Amata watched as the servant went under for the last time. She felt dizzy and sick to her stomach. Grabbing on to the side of the boat for support, she leaned over and retched into the Nile.

———

The rest of the trip proved uneventful. At the Theban palace Amata politely admired Miut's beautiful gowns and beaded glass jewelry, but she stayed clear of Miut's wrath. When one of the younger princesses accidentally broke Miut's favorite beaded necklace, Princess Miut mercilessly beat the girl with a stick. Since the young girl was the daughter of Pharaoh's fifth wife, no one seemed to notice.

———

At sunset on their last evening in Thebes, Amata strolled out into the garden on the northern end of the palace. Red and white camellias lined the pathway. Amata followed them out to a stone ledge that encircled a fountain. She sat down and hoped that the soothing sounds of the moving water would calm her tumultuous thoughts.

When Amata's tutor first explained to her the concept of *neheh*, the idea of intersecting what was seen with the unseen intrigued her. Now, however, she wasn't so sure. Did all Egyptian leaders believe they must maintain order in their society at the expense of human kindness and dignity? Princess Miut and her mother seemed to think so. Miut's angry outbursts frightened her. She enjoyed Miut's attention, especially since her own father, Balashi, seemed to have forgotten her. But did she really want such a hot-tempered friend?

"Well, good evening." A young man's voice startled Amata. She looked up and saw Prince Merib standing over her.

Amata rose and bowed. "Good evening, Prince Merib."

23

"May I sit next to you?" The prince gestured toward the stone ledge.

"But of course."

After they both took a seat, Prince Merib apologized. "I'm sorry I startled you. You looked deep in thought."

"I guess I was."

"And what deep thoughts would occupy the friend of my half-sister, Princess Miut?"

Amata knew that sixteen-year-old Princess Miut, daughter of Pharaoh's second wife, did not care much for eighteen-year-old Prince Merib, son of Pharaoh's first wife. She decided to change the subject. "We haven't seen much of you these past few days here in Thebes, Prince Merib. If I may be so bold, what has occupied your time here?"

Merib laughed. "I've been warned that you ask many questions, but yes, I will answer. I've been on a hunting expedition with my bodyguards the past few days."

"And did you catch anything?"

"Only your attention this evening."

Amata felt her face grow warm. She was a foreigner, and four years younger than Prince Merib. Surely he wasn't flirting with her, was he?

"I'm sorry; I hope I haven't made you feel uncomfortable."

"Well, maybe a little."

"Let's talk about something else. Have you heard that many of the nomarchs fear foreigners are taking over too many of our Egyptian businesses?"

Amata shifted her position on the stones. "Prince Merib, you know *I'm* a foreigner, don't you?"

"Right." The prince kicked a small pebble off the stone path. "I'm afraid I've blundered again. Well, what would you like to talk about? Anything."

"Really?"

Merib smiled. "Really."

Amata took in a quick breath. "Well, our cook, Eshe, says many of the administrative nomarchs in lower Egypt have grown corrupt. They care more about power and wealth than the wellbeing of their charges. She also says that many of them are trying to marry above their class and are building tombs in their own cities rather than in the Valley of the Kings, hoping to bolster their own local status. Is that true? If so, what does that mean for the future of Egypt?"

Merib's eyes opened a little wider. "You do speak your mind, don't you?"

Amata smiled and looked down. "You said I could talk about anything."

Merib sighed. "Well, the nomarchs didn't used to be so greedy. Until recently, they always upheld our Egyptian belief in an ordered society where everyone fulfills his duty and is satisfied with his station in life. Lately, however, I too have become aware of lower officials building their own tombs in their home cities instead of in the sacred cities. I realize they are doing this to strengthen their own local power. I'm also aware of the unauthorized cutbacks in food allotments and missing shipments of goods that should go to the people under the nomarchs' care."

Amata looked up and gazed at the prince's high cheekbones and chiseled jaw line. "Then why don't you do something about it?"

Merib shook his head. "I'm not Pharaoh. It's not my responsibility."

"Well, maybe it should be." Amata bit her lower lip, fearing she had said too much.

Merib stood and extended her his hand. "I think it's time to go now."

FIVE

On the boat ride home Amata didn't see much of Merib, and she interacted with Miut as little as possible. When they neared the docks at the port of Peru-Nefer Amata hurried to disembark. She barely noticed the squawking seagulls overhead, or the faint smell of saltwater beyond the Delta. She ached to talk with her father, but knew he probably wasn't home. As she stepped onto the pier, she caught a glimpse of two bearded, bare-chested young men with reddish-brown skin. They pushed heavy crates onto an anchored Phoenician boat. One of the crates broke apart and the crash startled her. Not looking where she stepped, Amata slipped off the dock and into the Nile.

One of the bearded young men dove in after her and dragged her to safety.

"Are you all right?" the young man asked as he sat her on the wooden pier.

Amata wiped beads of water from her face and began to shiver with cold. "I think so." She looked up at the muscled young man who had rescued her. "Thank you for pulling me out."

The young man looked over at a man near the curved Phoenician vessel. "Cousin, throw me a blanket."

Amata noticed that both men had short, dark brown beards and full heads of dark, curly hair. Even though they worked shirtless and wore kilts, she knew they weren't Egyptian. The young man's cousin walked over and tossed her rescuer a blanket.

Her rescuer wrapped the blanket around Amata. "I'm Urumilki, but you can call me Uru. I'm a trader from the Mediterranean port city of Gubal." Uru briskly rubbed

Amata's shoulders with the blanket to warm her. "Are you always in the habit of throwing yourself into the Nile so that handsome young men can rescue you?"

In spite of the cold, Amata laughed. "I'm afraid this is all your fault," she teased.

Uru's mouth dropped open in what Amata took as mock offense. "Excuse me, young lady. My cousin's the one who dropped the crate that must have distracted you. I am the one who jumped in to save you."

Amata looked over at Uru's cousin who was picking up the merchandise that had fallen out of the damaged crate. "And I do thank you, kind sir." Amata nodded in feigned decorum. "However, I must return to my group. I'm traveling with Princess Miut, I'll have you know." Amata felt a strange tingling when she looked into Uru's dark brown eyes. She enjoyed their banter.

Uru's eyes twinkled as he returned her gaze. "I should have known that such a beautiful young lady would be traveling with royalty. And here I am, just a lowly Phoenician." Uru helped Amata to her feet. "I will only release you into the care of the princess if you accept a small gift from me for causing you to fall into the Nile."

Amata laughed. "I was only teasing. I know it wasn't your fault. I didn't watch where I was going."

Uru lightly grasped Amata's forearm. "No, I insist." He turned to his cousin and shouted once again. "Barak. Bring me one of the alabaster jars from our shipment. One that's not broken. It's the least we can do for causing this unfortunate accident."

Amata protested. "Really, there's no need."

Uru pressed a finger to her lips. "I won't hear another word. These are very old alabaster jars that we planned to sell in our homeland, but I think you would appreciate one of them much more than the girls back home."

Barak handed Uru a small alabaster jar. "Fortunately," Barak told Uru, "most of the merchandise is undamaged."

Amata noticed that Barak's voice sounded deeper than Uru's voice. The lines in Barak's face made him look about twenty years old. Amata guessed from looking at Uru's softer face that he was about seventeen. With one hand, Amata grasped the blanket draped over her shoulders. With the other, she took the jar Uru offered her.

Just then Amata saw Princess Miut step off the boat and onto the docks. "Amata dear," the princess called out. "You really shouldn't talk with foreign traders when you are in my company. Come along now."

Amata bristled at Miut's condescending remark.

Uru released Amata's arm. She shrugged off the blanket in an effort to return it, but he wrapped it around her once more.

"No, keep it." Uru's eyes locked onto hers. "You can return it the next time I see you."

Amata's eyebrows rose. "If there is a next time."

When Amata arrived home, she was surprised to see her father eating the evening meal with Sam. She considered apologizing for not asking permission to go on the trip with Princess Miut, but then she felt her chest expand with anger. She was old enough to make her own decisions. Why should she have to ask permission? No. She'd just take her belongings to her room without saying a word. Then her father's voice stopped her.

"I'm so glad you are home, Amata. Please, won't you join us for the evening meal?"

Amata glanced at the extra plate on the table they had set for her. Sam sat with his head over his plate, pushing his cooked lentils around with his flatbread.

Amata saw a pleading look behind her father's eyes. How long had it been since they enjoyed a meal together? Then she saw disapproving lines crease her father's forehead as his eyes took in the black kohl outlining her eyes and the green malachite coloring her eyelids.

Suddenly Sam looked up and noticed her damp hair. "Amata, what happened to you?" He laughed. "Did you fall into the Nile on the way home?"

Amata's eyes narrowed. "As a matter of fact, yes."

The creases in Balashi's forehead deepened. "You left with only a note. It was wrong of you to leave without asking permission."

Amata raised her chin. "If I had, would you have granted it?"

Balashi shook his head. "I don't think it is wise for you to spend so much time with the princess and her family. And you fell into the Nile? Do you realize how dangerous that is?"

Amata felt her *wadjet*-framed eyes widen. "Perhaps not as dangerous as meeting the person who pulled me out." She knew her cryptic statement would only widen the growing gulf between them, but she didn't care. She glanced at her place setting, then at her father and Sam. "I'm not hungry," she finally announced. Tucking the belongings she had tied up in her linen cloth more firmly underneath her arm, she scurried off to her room.

SIX

The next morning Amata accompanied their cook, Eshe, to the market at the port of Peru-Nefer. Amata wanted to buy some fresh fruit. At least, that's what she told herself. As they neared the docks, she saw the Phoenician sailor, Barak, unloading cargo from his ship. She found herself searching for his cousin, Uru, who had pulled her from the Nile the previous day.

"Eshe," Amata said. "Would you see if the fruit seller at the end of the stalls has any figs or grapes? And don't come back until you find some coconuts."

"Coconuts?" Eshe's eyebrows raised. "You have never asked for coconuts. They are very hard to find."

Amata smiled. "If anyone can find them, I'm sure you can. I'll be looking at cloth over there." Amata pointed to a stall near the docks.

Amata walked the short distance to Uru and Barak's ship. Oars protruded from the boat's curved sides. A continuous line of planking stretched from stem to stern, probably, she thought, to protect the cargo from washing overboard during rough seas. The morning sun flashed in Amata's eyes when she gazed at the masts with their large yardarms and webbed rigging.

She saw Barak look up at her after unloading a large clay jar. He paused to rub his bearded face. "Ahh, the beautiful water lily my cousin recently plucked from the Nile. What brings you here today?"

Amata hadn't thought about what she'd say if she encountered Barak or Uru. "I, I," she stammered. Then she heard a voice behind her.

"Come to return my blanket?"

Amata turned and saw Uru carrying a heavy-looking clay jar on his bare shoulder. Two other men followed, also carrying jars. Amata felt her face blush. "I thought you didn't want the blanket back," she managed to say.

Uru laughed. "I don't. Besides. I see you didn't even bring it. Perhaps you came to take another dip in the Nile so I can save you again?"

Amata raised her chin. "No. I . . . ." She paused to gather her thoughts. "I just came to make sure you were all right." Amata dug her nails into her palms. Yesterday she felt so relaxed with Uru. What made her so flustered today?

Uru hefted the jar from his shoulder to Barak's. Amata watched as Barak and the other two men loaded their containers onto the ship.

Uru wiped sweat from his forehead with the back of his arm. "Actually, I wouldn't mind another dip. How about you?"

Uru took a threatening step toward Amata. She shrieked and held up her hands. "Don't you dare!"

Uru laughed. "Well, if not a swim, then how about a walk? We could get something to eat from a seller. I'm hungry." Uru caught a colorful linen cloth that Barak tossed him and slung it over his left shoulder.

At least the cloth covered part of Uru's bare copper chest. Amata knew Eshe would not approve if she saw her walking with a man, and neither would her father. But right now, she didn't care. Just walking next to him made her feel so alive.

Uru picked up a thick loaf of bread at the nearest stall and removed the ceramic scarab-shaped seal that hung around his neck. "So," Uru turned to Amata, "I know you are a friend of Princess Miut. What else can you tell me about yourself?"

Amata watched as the seller took Uru's blue-green ceramic seal and pressed it into wet clay. She knew that, since the Egyptians didn't have their own currency, many of the traders paid for goods with credit, bartering, or other coins from their own countries. Once Uru's scarab-shaped seal with the image of a bull on it appeared on the seller's clay, Uru replaced the seal's cord around his neck. He took his bread and led Amata over to a stall that sold vases and jars.

"That seller trusts you enough to let you pay with a seal?" Amata remarked.

"My cousin and I have traded at this port for the past five years. I've grown to love these people even more than my own." Uru walked over to the cloth seller and Amata followed. Uru picked up an embroidered linen and handed it to Amata.

"It's beautiful," she said, fingering the colorfully sewn stitches.

"This was made in the Canaanite port city of Gubal, my birthplace. It's one of the many items my cousin and I trade here, along with wine, bronzeworks, and timber from the forests of Lebanon. In return, we take back copper, gemstones, ivory, papyrus."

"And alabaster jars," Amata interrupted. She handed the cloth back to the merchant.

"How much for the linen?" Uru asked the seller.

"For you, one *deben*," the merchant replied.

"Het, that's how much it cost you to buy it from me," Uru protested. Amata watched as Uru drew hieroglyphs for two sacks of wheat onto Het's tablet of wet clay, and then pressed his scarab beetle seal onto the tablet. "I will return later this afternoon to pay you two *deben*—two sacks of wheat."

Het's smile revealed several broken teeth. The elderly man then grasped Uru's wrist. "Remember my offer to sell you my business. Have you thought more about it? I want to make sure my family is well cared for when I exchange this life for the next."

Uru chuckled. "You know I could never abandon the sea, or my cousin. And Het, I don't think you'll be leaving this life very soon. You have too much to live for."

Het continued to hold Uru's wrist. "May Ra look favorably upon you. You've always been kind to me and my humble family." The seller then released his grasp, bowed, and handed Uru the cloth.

Uru pressed the linen into Amata's hands. "For you, friend of Princess Miut."

Amata looked down at the cloth and shook her head. "No, I couldn't."

Uru curved Amata's fingers around the fine linen. "I insist. The price is that you must tell me your name and something about yourself."

Amata pulled the cloth to her chest. "Well, thank you." She dared herself to look into Uru's soft brown eyes. "It's beautiful. You are most generous." When she saw Uru staring back at her, she lowered her eyes. "I am Amata-sukkal, but you may call me Amata. I am the daughter of the Babylonian healer, Balashi." Amata looked up once again. "Now you must tell me more about yourself. You bought this cloth back from a merchant at twice its given price. Why would you do such a thing?"

Uru shrugged his shoulders. "As I said, I love the Egyptian people."

Uru led Amata to a booth displaying exquisite works of bronze and picked up a bronze knife that lay on a merchant's table. "Do you know that the Egyptians do not use death as a punishment?" Uru turned the knife over in his hand. "If an Egyptian judge deems someone worthy of death, the convicted man is forced to take his own life, usually by ingesting a lethal poison. Life is very sacred to the Egyptians."

Amata drank in the warmth she saw in Uru's brown eyes.

Uru returned the knife to the table. Amata then saw his eyes darken. "The Egyptians' view of life is not at all like that of my own people. For them, killing is just an everyday part of life."

Amata and Uru chatted their way through the market as the sun slowly climbed higher in the sky. Amata saw Eshe protectively watching from a safe distance. Amata flashed their servant a grateful smile for allowing her some privacy.

Amata told Uru about her father and Sam, and that they were in Egypt for a year of study to learn about Egyptian medical practices. She explained that when they returned to Babylon, Balashi and Sam would share what they learned with the Babylonian physicians. Amata found it easy to talk with Uru. She shared how her father's obsession to find the cause of her mother's death, and to hopefully find a cure, was ruining her relationship with her father. In return, she learned that Uru's parents were killed in a battle that Gubal had with a neighboring city when Uru was eight. Raised by his father's brother, Uru and Barak were more like brothers than cousins. Although Uru was four years younger, Amata sensed that Uru felt responsible for his older cousin.

"Barak doesn't look for trouble," Uru explained, "but trouble always seems to find him. He's been close to losing his father's trading business several times because of his hot head, and his tendency to make deals that promise great rewards with little effort. In fact, I've probably been gone too long from him already. By now he's probably traded his father's boat for a non-existent gold mine."

As they slowly walked back toward the ship, Amata asked, "Do you think you'll always be a trader? Does that merchant's offer to buy his business tempt you in any way?"

Uru looked out over the waters and sighed. "The sea is all I know. I love the fresh ocean breeze and the salty air." Uru turned and grasped Amata's hand. "Although, I do hope to have a family some day."

Amata felt her face burn. She couldn't think of anything to say.

Uru laughed. "I didn't mean to embarrass you. I suppose one day I will find a nice Egyptian girl or else a Phoenician woman to settle down with." Uru's eyes twinkled. "Or perhaps I'll have a beautiful woman at each port as I conduct my trade between Egypt and Canaan. How would they know?"

Amata loved the way his grin deepened the dimples in his cheeks. He looked so adorable that she could almost kiss him. Instead, she punched him in the arm, something she always did when teased by Sam. "That's disgusting," she shot back. "They would know. Women always know."

Uru looked deeply into Amata's eyes. "I suppose they do."

SEVEN

The morning after Amata returned from her trip up the Nile River, Sam and Balashi resumed their studies in the House of Scrolls. Sam found it hard to concentrate. He started to ask Balashi for the day off so that he and Amata could explore the hidden tomb, but then a palace messenger arrived asking to see Qar, the Chief Physician. Sam watched as the messenger spoke with Qar in hushed tones. The Chief Physician then consulted with the administrative scribe, Iny. Nakthor was nowhere in sight.

Iny almost shouted at Qar. "Yes, yes. Go immediately. And take the foreigners with you."

Sam almost tripped several times as he hobbled behind Balashi and Qar on their way out of the palmwood paneled House of Scrolls.

"We must keep this quiet," Sam heard Qar tell Balashi. "The Priest of Ptah has fallen ill." The two men rushed down the dusty, columned-lined road that led out of the sacred compound. Sam trailed behind them. Once they passed the Temple of Ptah and the House of Life, Qar finally slowed his pace.

"What are the Priest of Ptah's symptoms?" Balashi asked Qar.

Qar lowered his voice. "The High Priest of Ptah, head of all clergy in Memphis, grew ill last night while visiting with Pharaoh. Nakthor is already at the palace chanting sacred texts over him. We've been summoned to the winter residence to see what more we can do. They say that, before this, the high priest's throat had burned for several days, and he had stomach pains. Then he had difficulty breathing. Last night and this morning he's continued to have violent stomach pains followed by vomiting and an extreme need to continually empty his intestines.

Sam leaned on his walking stick. "Has the high priest been given the white powder derived from calcite to soothe his stomach?"

Balashi laid a hand on Sam's head. "This sounds like much more than a mere stomach ailment, Sam."

Qar nodded. "Yes, much more. In fact, I suspect he's been poisoned."

When they reached Pharaoh's winter palace, guards escorted them through the columned portico that stood in front of the immense limestone-walled northern gate. Once inside, they wove their way through massive hallways where large circular papyri-shaped stone columns tapered to uphold the expansive ceiling.

A servant ushered them into a bedchamber where the high priest lay moaning on a bed. Just as they entered, the Priest of Ptah vomited into a pan on the floor.

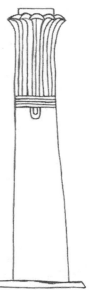

Sam distracted himself by looking up at the high ceiling decorated with tiles of small turquoise squares outlined by cream-colored swirls. He also glanced at the walls ornamented with painted tiles of river plants and noticed how the wall torches cast eerie shadows on them. He admired how the tall pillars that lined the sides of the room re-sembled bundled reeds. The stone columns' fluted tops, inlaid with varied-colored glazes, sported gilded capitals where the pillars met the ceiling.

Balashi grasped the high priest's wrist and felt for a pulse. "Something must be blocking one of the channels from his heart. The blood moving through his body is very slow and erratic."

The High Priest of Ptah pounded his fists on the bed. "Blasphemy! Remove this foreigner from my room. Certainly the gods are angry with me. Have Nakthor repeat the sacred texts." The Priest of

Ptah clutched his stomach and vomited again. "Nakthor. Where are you?"

Sam glanced at the bamboo nightstand where a blue-glazed ceramic water pitcher stood. He saw white dust surrounding its base. Someone must have already given the high priest the calcite powder. Obviously, it hadn't helped. Sam sidled over to the table, wet his finger, and took a sample of the white powder. He touched his finger to his tongue. Instead of getting the sour, bitter taste he expected, the powder left a metallic taste in his mouth.

Just then, Nakthor walked through the chamber's large, colorfully framed doorway. His long white belted tunic billowed around him. His bony clean-shaven head darted left then right as he assessed those assembled in the room. "Qar, why did you bring the foreigners here? Out, out!" He beat the air as if to shoo away a fly.

Qar motioned to a servant standing at the foot of the bed. "Please take Balashi and the lad to the courtyard balcony. I will join them soon."

Once Sam and Balashi were alone on the balcony, Sam blurted out, "The Priest of Ptah was poisoned. I'm sure of it!"

For a few moments, Balashi peered out over the marbled railing and studied the beautiful flower garden below. Slowly he turned to Sam. "And what makes you so sure?"

Sam glanced around, and then spoke softly. "Before we arrived, Qar said he suspected poisoning. And did you see the white powder at the base of the water pitcher? I thought it was calcium powder, but it didn't taste like it. It tasted like metal."

Balashi stroked his beard. "White powder that tastes like metal. I don't suppose you were able to gather a sample of it."

"No, we had to leave too quickly. But I left my medicine pouch in the room so I'd have an excuse to go back later."

Balashi stroked his beard again and watched as the garden below filled with young women dressed in white ankle-length gowns. Sam noticed that each girl carried some sort of musical instrument.

Balashi inhaled deeply. "It's possible that someone poisoned the High Priest of Ptah with antimony sulfide powder. If so, there's nothing we can do about it."

From his studies, Sam knew that antimony sulfide was often used in making kohl. Its white powder was ground up with other substances, such as hardened sap from the acacia trees to help solidify the paste, and frankincense to add a sweet, woody fragrance. When mixed with animal fat and burnt, the resulting soot was then mixed with liquid to create the black kohl. Both male and female Egyptians used the black eyeliner when painting the falcon god's symbol of the *wadjet* around their eyes. As Sam had read in the scrolls, small doses of the white antimony sulfide powder, taken internally over time, would result in death. Was the Priest of Ptah poisoned by antimony sulfide? If so, who had access to it, and why would they target the Priest of Ptah?

Qar soon joined them out on the balcony. As the Chief Physician talked quietly with Balashi, Sam's thoughts turned to the girls gathered below. A few sang softly as they played their harps or lyres. Sam leaned over a little more and saw Princess Miut talking with one of her servants. In one hand the princess held what looked like Keret's alabaster jar.

Just then an Egyptian servant interrupted Qar and Balashi's conversation. "Great Physician," the servant addressed Qar. "Come quickly. The Priest of Ptah has died."

EIGHT

As news of the priest's death spread, the winter palace burst into a flurry of activity. Sam hoped to get back into the bedroom chamber to retrieve his medicine bag and to take a sample of the powder left on the nightstand, but Nakthor demanded that Sam and Balashi leave the palace immediately. On their way out, a messenger informed them that their services were urgently needed at the house of Fenuku. The Chief Sculptor had taken a turn for the worse.

Keret greeted Sam and Balashi at the door of his master's home. Keret's red-rimmed eyes and unkempt hair told their own story. "You're too late. Fenuku just breathed his last."

Balashi elbowed his way past Keret. Sam went into the cooking courtyard with Keret while a servant prepared the evening meal.

Keret hung his head and looked down at the sandy dirt floor. "Near the end, every breath grew more and more labored," Keret explained. "I felt so helpless. Fenuku was the only family I knew. Now he's gone. What will I do?"

Sam felt a burning in his chest. It was the same helpless feeling he got when Amata had a problem he couldn't fix.

Keret looked at Sam with glistening eyes. "I want to show you something."

Keret led Sam to his own bedchambers. On the wall next to his sleeping pallet stood a polished limestone statue that stood as tall as Keret. Sam recognized it as a statue of Ptah, the creator-god of Memphis.

"A year ago, Fenuku sculpted this statue of Ptah and gave it to me as a present. He told me it would serve as protection if anything ever happened to him." Keret fingered the statue's detailed hands that grasped a *was* scepter, an *ankh* symbol, and a *djed* pillar. From the lessons Amata had learned and shared with Sam, he knew that the *was, ankh,* and *djed* represented three of Egypt's highest values: life, power and stability.

Sam admired the lifelike image and the intricate details of the statue. "Fenuku was an amazing sculptor," he commented.

"That's not all." Keret squeezed behind the statue, braced his back against the bedroom's limestone wall, and, pushing with his feet and hands, inched the statue forward. The newly exposed space between the statue and the wall revealed a hidden panel near the base of the floor.

"Fenuku also taught me the art of creating secret panels." Keret stood and tugged on a decorative bronze bracket that secured a torch lamp on the wall next to the statue. The hidden panel slid open. "I made this small chamber six months ago. It was my first. Since then, Fenuku let me help him with several more, including some in Pharaoh's winter palace."

Keret reached inside the secret compartment and withdrew several stone *shabti* figures. Most of the small figures held stone working tools such as a chisel, hammerstone, or drill. "I made these *shabtis* to accompany Fenuku in the afterlife." Keret laid the miniature servants out on his sleeping pallet.

Sam noticed hieroglyphs inscribed on the *shabtis'* legs. He remembered Amata telling him that the Egyptian word *shabti* meant answerer. The inscriptions were spells that informed each *shabti* of its job. Egyptians believed that the god Osiris had public works projects for the Egyptians to do in the afterlife. They believed that if they had *shabtis* with them in their tomb, then the *shabtis* would perform this work for them.

Keret reached through the opening a little further and gently withdrew a folded linen cloth. He then placed the cloth on his bed and opened it. Inside the cloth laid several gold bracelets. One was decorated with lapis lazuli, another with irregularly shaped turquoise beads, and a third had a single hollow gold rosette in the center. "Fenuku received these as gifts throughout the years," Keret explained. "He told me to keep them until I turned eighteen. He said I could do whatever I wanted with them after I turned eighteen because he would grant me my freedom then." Keret also withdrew a sheet of papyrus from the cloth. "A week before he died, Fenuku ordered a scribe to draw up this will. It states that, upon his death, Fenuku grants my freedom. All that he owned is now mine."

Sam picked up one of the *shabti* and looked at it more closely. "So what will you do now? Return to Canaan?"

Keret put the jewelry and will back into the cloth and refolded it. "I don't know anyone in Canaan. I was sold to Fenuku when I was eight. Without Fenuku, I don't really feel like I belong anywhere. For now, I guess I'll continue to work here in Memphis as a sculptor. Perhaps one day Pharaoh will appoint me as Chief Sculptor." A faint smile flicked across Keret's face. "And now that I am a free man, perhaps I can gather enough wealth to pursue Princess Miut."

Sam handed the *shabti* back to Keret and watched his friend return the figurines and cloth package to their compartment. Sam knew what it felt like not to belong. After his mother and brother died, Sam thought he'd never know the love of a family again. If anything ever happened to Balashi or Amata—Sam refused to finish his thought.

Sam also pushed away thoughts of telling Keret that he saw Princess Miut with Keret's alabaster jar. Sam suspected that Nakthor had recently given the jar to the princess as a gift, perhaps as a courting gesture. Sam shuddered to think of the young princess marrying Nakthor, a man almost twice her age. What if the princess eventually became heir to Egypt's throne? Would Nakthor then become Pharaoh?

Sam put the thought out of his mind. "You mentioned that you and Fenuku created secret panels in the royal palace. Was that at Pharaoh's request, or are you not allowed to talk about it?"

"Actually, recently Princess Miut and her mother asked us to create a secret panel connecting the princess's room to the adjoining room."

Sam's eyebrows rose.

"I had planned to talk to you about that," Keret said. "The princess and her mother said they heard rumors of assassination plots against Pharaoh and some of the royal family members. We finished Princess Miut's panel just a few days ago."

"Who would want to kill the royal family?" Sam asked.

"I don't know," Keret replied, "but you might want to warn Amata to be careful when she visits the princess at the palace. Better yet, maybe Balashi should order her to stay away from the palace."

"Hmph," Sam responded. "Like that would do any good."

Before long, Balashi came out of Fenuku's room and sent some of Fenuku's servants to notify Nakthor and the palace officials of Fenuku's death. When funerary priests arrived, they took Fenuku's body to a purification tent to prepare it for embalming. Keret told Sam that the palace was paying for Fenuku's embalming and burial in a tomb reserved for palace craftsmen. Since Sam and Balashi were no longer needed, they went back to the House of Scrolls.

———————

As Sam and Balashi walked home later that evening, Sam decided not to say anything to Balashi about Keret's warnings. At least, not yet. "Do you think things have calmed down enough now at the palace?" Sam asked. "I need to go back and get my medicine bag."

"Perhaps," Balashi replied. "But if Nakthor is there, do your best to avoid him. Dealing with two deaths in one day may have left him in a very foul mood."

Sam glanced over at his adoptive father and saw that he walked slower than usual. Sam stopped and laid a hand on Balashi's arm. For the first time, he noticed Balashi's stooped shoulders and listless eyes. "Father, why don't you go home to eat and get some rest. I'm sure Eshe has a wonderful meal ready for us. I'll be along in a while."

Balashi didn't argue.

Moments later, Sam found himself back at the palace.

NINE

As Sam neared the northern gate of Pharaoh's winter palace, he saw Amata and Princess Miut approaching, along with the princess's younger half-sisters and their mothers. Bodyguards flanked the small entourage.

Amata quickly walked over to Sam. "What are you doing here?" she whispered.

The tightness in Amata's voice made Sam feel like an outsider. "We were summoned to help with the Priest of Ptah earlier today," Sam explained, "but the priest died. I accidentally left my medicine bag here and came back to get it."

"Well, it's a good thing we arrived when we did." Amata quickly glanced back at Princess Miut and the others who were a short distance behind her. "How did you expect to get into the palace without an escort?"

Sam hadn't thought about that. "Well, since you're here, I guess I don't have to worry about that now, do I?"

Amata rolled her eyes and gave Sam an annoyed sigh. "The princess, her half-sisters and I are performing in a concert for Pharaoh this evening. I'd appreciate it if you went in and came out as quickly as possible."

Amata walked over to Miut's bodyguards. After a brief exchange, the guards nodded, bowed, and gestured for Sam to follow them into the palace.

Amata and the princess went into Miut's chambers while a guard escorted Sam to the room where the Priest of Ptah had died. Princess Miut's room was right next to it. Sam saw the guard take up a position outside his doorway. Sam hurried over to the nightstand and found his bag underneath it. Sprinkles of the white powder still lay on

44

top of the nightstand. Sam began to sweep the powder into a small pouch inside his bag when he heard Princess Miut call out for the guard. A few minutes later he heard the girls' sandals pattering down the large hallway.

"Yes," he heard Miut's voice call out. "We need you to escort us to the music room. I'm sure the boy can find his own way out."

———— • ————

Amata wet her dry lips and silently fingered the strings of her lyre. She glanced at the visitors who now filled the music room and spotted at least ten shaved heads. She knew they belonged to important priests. At first, the little concert was only intended for Pharaoh and his family. Somehow it had grown into a much larger event. Amata wasn't playing any solos, only group ensembles with Princess Miut and her half-sisters. Reminding herself of that fact, however, didn't keep her stomach from doing flips or her fingers from vibrating like the strings of her lyre.

In front of the group of priests sat Nakthor and his administrative assistant, Iny. Pharaoh sat on a raised platform in a gilded wooden chair that faced the small crowd. Prince Merib sat on his right, and Merib's mother sat on Pharaoh's left. The *wadjet* of Horus decorated their eyes. Amata marveled at the splendor  of Pharaoh's clothing. The thin flaxen robe worn over his kilt, the leopard skin draped over his shoulders, and the golden armbands and necklace embedded with precious stones all spoke of his wealth and honored position. This was the first time Amata had seen Pharaoh, and she was particularly struck with the regal yellow and black-striped *nemes* head cloth he wore on his head. From her angle just below him, she saw that the *nemes* extended a little down his back and had two large flaps that hung down behind his ears before reappearing in front of both shoulders.

The din of voices in the music room quieted immediately when Pharaoh stood. His deep voice filled the room.

"I have called everyone here on such short notice because of the recent deaths of the Priest of Ptah and the Chief Sculptor. These deaths are a great loss to our kingdom."

Amata looked over at Nakthor and saw a crooked smile form on his face.

With palms up, Pharaoh slightly raised his arms in front of him. "Now that their *ka*, their life force, has left the bodies of the Priest of Ptah and the Chief Sculptor, their physical remains have been taken to the *ibu* tents for purification by the embalmers. I am sure that when Anubis leads them to the Hall of Two Truths they will both pass the scrutiny of the forty-two judges and the gods. I am also assured that when Anubis weighs their hearts, each will prove lighter than the feather of truth, and that their *ba*, their eternal, true inner selves, will reunite with their *ka*."

Amata thought about the day she first met the Chief Sculptor in his shop. She had learned about Egyptian religious beliefs regarding the afterlife, but she never applied them to someone she knew. She tried to imagine the jackal-faced  god, Anubis, weighing the sculptor's heart. She knew that if it weighed more than the feather of truth, his heart would be devoured by the jaws of Ammut. If that happened, the sculptor's *ka* and his *ba* would never reunite. She conjured up an image of Ammut, the crocodile-headed demoness with the body of a leopard and backside of a hippopotamus. Her tutor had sketched the creature on papyrus for her when she asked him to describe it. The vision of Ammut's jaws chomping down on a human heart made her shudder. *When I die, will I survive the weighing of my heart? Can anyone?*

Pharaoh now lowered his arms and spoke about Osiris ushering the departed's reunited *ba* and *ka* into the Land of Two Fields, the true Egypt of the gods. Amata wondered if Pharaoh gave this kind of lecture after the death of every great servant, or if today was special. She scanned the room, searching for other familiar faces. She saw Keret looking in her direction. *Why is he here?* Amata then glanced at Princess Miut and saw that she and Keret had their eyes locked onto each other. Amata looked away and focused again on Pharaoh.

"As your representative of the gods here in this earthly life," Pharaoh continued, "the appointment of a new Priest of Ptah falls upon me. This position is especially important here in Memphis where we honor Ptah as the god who first conceived the world."

Pharaoh raised his arms once again. "As it says in the sacred texts, 'He who made all and created the gods, he is Ta-tenen, the creator god Ptah, who gave birth to the gods, and from whom everything came forth. Thus Ptah was satisfied after he made all things and all divine words.'" Pharaoh paused, lowered his arms again, and looked out over the audience. He pointed a finger in Nakthor's direction. "To fulfill the position of Priest of Ptah, I have chosen the lector-priest, Nakthor."

Amata saw Iny smile as Nakthor slowly rose from his seat and bowed low toward Pharaoh.

"And," Pharaoh continued, "the position of Master Sculptor must also receive special consideration. Since Ptah is responsible for the creation of the universe by his thought and by his word, he is also the patron, the protector and guardian of craftsmen. Therefore, I have not chosen to grant the position of Master Sculptor to Fenuku's apprentice and former slave, known by the name of Keret. Instead, I grant the title of Master Sculptor to Rahotep, another fine sculptor who will be able to complete the last projects assigned to Master Sculptor Fenuku, including the new temple statue of Ptah. The sculptor Keret will now work under the authority of Chief Sculptor Rahotep."

Amata saw a tall, muscular man, whom she assumed was Rahotep, stand and bow low. She stole a look at Keret. He still only had eyes for Miut. Amata couldn't tell how he felt about working under Rahotep.

Pharaoh announced several other new appointments, but something in the upper balcony at the back of the

room caught Amata's attention. She thought
she saw several guards stationed there, then a
flicker of shadows. When she looked again,
she saw no one.

Amata almost missed Pharaoh's com-
mand to begin the concert. Her fingers
fumbled a little, but she managed to play
most notes correctly. While Amata played
the lyre, Princess Miut played the harp,
and several of Miut's half-sisters played
bamboo flutes of varying lengths. They had
practiced their pieces for several weeks, and
Amata hoped the music pleased Pharaoh.

When they finished, Pharaoh simply
rose without so much as a nod. He turned and motioned
for his wife and Prince Merib to follow. Suddenly, Amata
felt a whiz of air zing past her ear. Prince Merib then
stumbled and fell to the ground. She saw the shaft of an
arrow protruding from his chest. Merib's mother screamed
and ran to her son. Princess Miut's half-sisters shrieked.
Instruments fell to the ground. Amata heard people scream
as they clamored to leave the room. Amata froze in place,
unable to move. Bodyguards raced to Pharaoh's platform
and formed a shield around the prince. Other guards
escorted Pharaoh and his wife to safety. One bodyguard
waved toward the upper balcony and shouted orders to
other soldiers to apprehend the shooter.

"Amata!" Princess Miut shook Amata's arm and then
pulled her to her feet. "Amata," she screamed again. "You
must leave immediately. The prince has been shot. He
might even be . . ."

Amata struggled to focus her eyes on Miut. "Yes," was
all she managed to say. Stunned by the violence, Amata
felt numb as she walked home alone.

After Sam heard the guards escort Princess Miut and
Amata to the music room to play Pharaoh's concert, Sam
waited a few more minutes just inside the doorway of the

Priest of Ptah's room. He then stuck his head out and glanced down the hallway. No other guards were in sight. He inhaled deeply, stepped back into the bedroom and looked around more carefully. Earlier that day he noticed torches dotting the walls. He looked at the walls again. The torches sat in bronze brackets similar to the ones he'd seen in Keret's bedroom.

Perhaps if he pulled on one of the brackets. Sam went to the wall and tugged downward on the cool metal. Nothing. He pulled another. Just as he hoped, a hidden panel slid open. Sam stepped forward and found himself in Princess Miut's chambers. Once inside the princess's room, he saw the same brackets and torches on her walls. He pulled one of these brackets and the panel slid shut.

The princess's beautifully carved cedar bed frame sat on a raised platform at one end of the room. Cedar chests placed against the far wall sported alabaster jars of various sizes, several copper mirrors, hairbrushes with wooden handles, and bone-toothed combs. He examined the alabaster jars more carefully and found one with a distinctive crack. Keret's jar. Sam lifted its knobbed lid. Inside he found white powder. Licking a finger, he sampled the powder. Just as he suspected, it left a metallic taste in his mouth. Either the princess poisoned the Priest of Ptah, or someone with access to her room had done the deed.

Sam examined the rest of the items in the room, careful to return everything to its original position. Suddenly he heard far-away shouts and then more distinct voices coming down the hallway. It didn't sound as if he had time to get to the other side of the room and escape through the panel before the voices reached him. Seeing a large clay jar filled with palm fronds in a nearby corner, Sam slipped behind it. He hoped the voices belonged to people who would simply pass by the room and continue down the hall. He was wrong.

"I'm so afraid. It's a good thing you were here."

Sam recognized the first voice as that of Princess Miut.

"Princess, you're shaking." To Sam's surprise, he realized the second voice belonged to Keret.

They had both entered the princess's room.

"Do you think Prince Merib will survive?" The princess sniffled.

"The arrow nearly missed his heart. I heard they caught the shooter immediately. It was one of his Nubian body-guards. Now tell me about the problem with your secret panel. You said it wasn't working correctly?"

Sam stood on his toes to peek through an opening between the palm fronds. As he adjusted his position, he didn't notice the princess's cat on the floor next to him. He accidentally stepped on its tail.

The cat let out a sharp "Mreow!" and skittered out from behind the large jar.

"What?" the princess cried out.

Unfazed, Keret walked over to the far wall and pulled on one of the brackets. The panel opened easily.

"I thought you said you had a problem with it," Keret said.

The princess seemed to forget about her cat. She ran over to Keret and wrapped her thin arms around him. "I only said that because I wanted to get you alone with me. I know you have feelings for me. Take me away from all of this. If they tried to kill Merib, I might be next."

Keret's hands remained at his sides. He towered over Miut as she laid her head against his chest. "Princess, please," Keret said. "This isn't proper. If someone sees us together in your bedchambers, I could lose my life. Your guards will keep you safe."

The princess began to cry. "I don't want the guards to keep me safe. I want you. Don't you understand?"

Sam saw Miut look up at Keret as she pulled his head toward hers and kissed him on the lips.

Keret slowly raised an arm and began to wrap it around her waist.

"What is the meaning of this?"

Sam heard a shout come from the direction of the bedroom door. He peered between the palm fronds and saw Nakthor stride into the princess's room.

Keret pushed Miut away from him.

"He was just repairing a wall," Miut explained.

"It looks to me like he breached a wall." Nakthor snickered. "I should have you arrested." Nakthor grabbed Keret's arm. "Come with me."

"Let me explain," Keret protested.

"Your actions are the only explanation I need."

Although he could have easily struggled free, Keret left with Nakthor. Sam watched the princess walk over to one of her cedar chests and pick up a brush and mirror. Looking into the mirror, she slowly brushed through her short black hair. A moment later, she left.

Sam waited, fearing he'd be caught in Miut's room. The image of Nakthor dragging Keret out burned in his mind. *What will happen to Keret now?*

When Sam no longer heard voices in the hallway, he quietly moved toward the secret panel and pulled on the bracket. The wall didn't open. Sam's hand quivered. He pulled on it again. Nothing. If he couldn't return through the panel, he'd have to go out the door. What if someone saw him coming out? Sam studied the wall more carefully and finally realized he'd pulled on the wrong bracket. He pulled on the torch holder to his left. To his relief, the panel slid back. He quickly stepped into the next room. After closing the panel he retrieved his medicine bag and left the palace.

TEN

Sam tore off a stray stalk of wheat that grew near his house and popped a kernel into his mouth. The kernel didn't have much moisture left. Soon the Season of Planting, *Peret*, would give way to *Shomu*, the season of harvest. Two months had passed since Merib's attempted assassination. Sam kicked a rock with his rush-woven sandal as he limped out to the field behind the house. He chastised himself for not having done more to heal the rift between Amata and Balashi. Five months had passed since they arrived in Egypt, and each day Amata seemed more distant. When they returned to Babylon in seven more months, would Amata want to go with them or remain in Egypt?

Sam looked down at the crunched stalk he now gripped in his hand. He didn't realize he'd squeezed his hand into a fist. In spite of the attempt on Prince Merib's life, Amata spent even more time with the royal family as the pharaoh alternately ruled from Thebes and then returned to take care of business in Memphis. When the pharaoh was in Memphis, Amata sailed south to Thebes with the princess and her family. Now, Amata never bothered to ask Balashi for permission. Usually she just left a message with their servant, Eshe.

Sam crunched the stalk again and tossed it aside as he approached one of their donkeys grazing in the field. He thought about Balashi. His adoptive father still hadn't found a cure for the illness that caused Fenuku's death. Each day Balashi grew more and more despondent and often sent Sam off alone to study at the House of Scrolls. "I need to stay home and tend to my herbs and fruit trees,"

Balashi would say. Sam saw that Balashi began to retire earlier at night and wake up later each morning.

Today when Balashi chose to stay home, Sam asked for permission to take the day off from his studies. Balashi agreed. Sam couldn't get the secret tomb out of his mind. He knew Nakthor was somehow involved. Over three months had passed since he and Amata visited the tomb near Giza. He'd hoped that Amata's sense of adventure would return and she'd help him uncover its mystery, but whenever he asked her about it, she simply said, "I'm too busy with the princess." And Balashi kept him working so hard that he didn't have time to go alone.

The early morning sun warmed Sam's back as he led one of the donkeys from the field to the house. He kicked another rock as his thoughts drifted back again to Amata. In addition to the time Amata spent with the princess, she also spent many mornings accompanying Eshe to the Delta where they bought fruits and vegetables. In a rare moment of conversation with Sam, Amata let it slip that she usually spent those mornings talking with a Phoenician trader named Uru, the one who had given her an old, small alabaster jar.

Sam could tell by the questions Amata asked him about Keret that she also secretly liked the young sculptor. However, Amata recently confided to Sam that lately Princess Miut seemed to have a claim on Keret, so even if Amata did like Keret, she didn't dare to show it. Instead, Amata explained, "I spend as much time as possible with Uru. He's a very good listener." Sam kicked another rock. Amata used to say that about him.

Sam felt an ache between his ribs as he recalled the carefree afternoons he and Amata once spent on Enlil's raft floating on the Euphrates River, sharing snippets of their past and hopes for the future. Those early days in Babylon felt as though they were more than just two years ago. At least Uru and his crew were now on their way to Phoenicia to sell the goods they recently bought in Egypt. As quickly as the thought entered Sam's mind, he berated himself for feeling jealous of Amata's friendship with the young sailor.

And what about Prince Merib? Sam believed he'd also detected a slight attraction between Amata and the prince. Amata seemed overly concerned with the prince's health after he was shot with an arrow, even though she denied any interest in him.

"I'm only concerned for the smooth transition of power in Egypt," she defended herself. "If anything happened to the prince, it would create instability throughout the country. I'm glad he recovered. I think he'll make a wise ruler some day."

The prince's would-be assassin, one of his bodyguards from Punt, was killed trying to escape capture. Fortunately, the assassin's arrow missed the prince's vital organs and, between Qar and Balashi's excellent care, Amata shared that Merib was now recuperating at the Theban palace. Was Merib's presence in Thebes the reason why Amata accompanied the princess up the Nile again this week?

Turning all of these thoughts over in his mind, and having received Balashi's permission to take a short trip to Giza, Sam began to tie his supplies onto the donkey. Balashi had recently purchased two donkeys, one for him and one for Balashi. Sam stopped to pat the donkey's neck. "I'm sure glad we don't have to walk everywhere now, old girl," he told the animal. The donkey lifted her head and brayed. Now that he and Balashi were getting calls to visit officials in the outlying regions, they needed a faster way to travel.

Remembering to take along warm coals and oil to provide light in the dark tomb, Sam also loaded the jenny with two goatskins of water, a bag of dried fish, and a bag of dried fruit. As always, he tapped beneath his tunic to make sure he had his bronze dagger.

With each jostling step of the donkey, Sam's heart beat a little faster. He put thoughts of Amata aside as he plodded on toward the hidden tomb. Swirls of dust and sand clawed at his face. He tied a cloth over his mouth and nose to keep from breathing in the grit. The morning sun felt hot, but at least a slight breeze rose from the direction of the Nile. Soon he reached the Delta where he stopped at Keret's workshop for a quick visit.

Not much had changed since he and Amata last saw Keret. The half of the shop where Keret worked looked the same. Sam guessed that the other area contained Rahotep's workspace. Tools such as hammerstones, a hollow copper drill, a copper saw, and copper and bronze chisels covered the Master Sculptor's worktable. Rahotep however, was no-where in sight.

"Where is Master Sculptor Rahotep?" Sam asked.

Keret chiseled and sanded what looked like a baldhead rising out of a piece of limestone before he looked up. "Rahotep's working in the sacred temple, putting the finishing touches on the new statue of Ptah." Keret wiped sweat from his forehead with the back of his hand. "Fenuku almost completed the project before he, before his *ka* left him, but now I suppose Rahotep will take all the credit for the statue."

Sam noticed an edge in Keret's voice. "You really miss Fenuku, don't you?"

Keret shrugged and returned to sanding the limestone head. "They say Fenuku's in a better place now. Supposedly his *ka* and his *ba* reunite with his body every evening. The priests say that during the day his *ba* watches over me, while his *ka* flies off to enjoy life in the eternal Land of Two Fields. Any work his *ka* is required to do there is carried out by the *shabtis* I made for him."

Sam kept quiet for a moment. He finally interjected, "It doesn't sound like you really believe that."

Keret finally looked up from his work. "I don't sense Fenuku watching over me. And I miss him so much, Sam. I'd give anything to have him back."

Sam saw Keret's eyes moisten, but Keret quickly looked down and went back to sculpting.

Sam changed the subject. "What are you working on?"

Keret laughed. "You mean you can't tell by looking at this big head? The new Priest of Ptah, Nakthor, tasked me with sculpting a statue of him. Between you and me, I don't think Nakthor's much of a priest. He cares more about power and position than he does about religion."

Sam had his own suspicions about Nakthor. He pressed Keret for more information. "So what do you know about Nakthor?"

Keret didn't look up. "I've said too much already. You'd better go before Rahotep returns or Nakthor comes to check on the progress of his precious statue."

Sam didn't give up. He changed the subject once more. "What about Princess Miut? How are things going with her? Now that you're a free man, do you think you and the princess might have a chance at being together like you've always wanted?"

Keret stopped sanding the statue's head and looked up. His eyes narrowed into slits. "Nothing," he growled, "nothing's going as planned, but I'm working to fix that. Now, if you don't mind, I've got work to do."

Sam turned and left. On the ride to the tomb, Sam thought over recent events. Did someone really poison the Priest of Ptah, as he suspected? If so, who poisoned him, and why? Did Keret play a part in any of this? He wished he could get his friend to open up. What happened between Keret and Nakthor after they left Princess Miut's room? Sam was afraid to tell Keret he'd witnessed the scene. With Amata and Balashi so distant recently, he didn't want to do anything that might jeopardize his friendship with Keret.

———

Sam reached the hidden tomb just before midday. He carefully placed his donkey's woven papyrus lead under a heavy rock and then found the boulder covering the opening. As he had previously done, Sam used his walking stick as leverage and managed to create an opening large enough to crawl through. Sam lit his lamp with the hot coals and entered the dark passageway.

Sam quickly found his way to the small room he first visited. This time the room contained no jars. It sat completely empty. Sam held up the lamp and studied the room's walls. Hieroglyphs of prayers, painted pictures of the gods, and elaborate stone torch sconces adorned the area. *There has to be more to this tomb. But what? Why were men sneaking in and out of it?*

Sam studied each wall again, moving more slowly this time. When he reached the back wall, he thought he detected a slight crack. On a whim, Sam pulled on one of the wall torch's brackets. Nothing. He walked a little further and pulled on another sconce bracket. This time the wall opened, revealing another, much larger room. In the middle of the room stood twelve tall clay jars. Sam quickly entered the larger room. Putting his lamp close to the top of the jars, he saw that each container was fastened shut and stamped with a seal in the shape of a scarab beetle. The outline of a bull was inscribed on the beetle's back.

He could break one of the jar's seals to see what was inside, but then whoever put the jars in the tomb would know their secret had been discovered. He bent down and held the lamp closer to the earthen floor and examined it more carefully. He saw bits of wheat covering a small area around one of the jars. Was someone stockpiling grain here?

Sam thought of the torch bracket he'd just used to gain access to this room. The bracket was just like the one in Princess Miut's room that opened the hidden entrance to the adjoining bedchamber. Keret said he'd made that secret panel. Did he also make this one? A chill suddenly ran through Sam's body. Was Keret so desperate to win Miut's hand in marriage that he would steal, store, and sell stolen grain to earn more money in order to gain her approval? Sam had no answers, but he felt certain Keret and Nakthor were somehow involved.

ELEVEN

Amata wandered out to the Theban palace garden and sat on the low granite wall surrounding the large circular pond. Bright red, yellow, and pink mums outlined the stone's enclosure. Blue and peach-colored water lilies with intense golden centers appeared to float on the water's surface. They opened up to the early morning sun, inviting it to caress their most inward parts. Amata wished the sun would also reach her inner recesses. She hoped that another trip to Thebes with the princess and her family would cheer her, but she hadn't experienced such pangs of loneliness since her mother died.

Whom did she have? Lately, her father and Sam seemed so distant. Uru would not return for at least another month, and Keret seemed beyond her reach. Princess Miut feigned interest in Keret, but she really only cared about clothes, jewels and power. Miut beat her slaves for the smallest mistakes. And when Merib recovered from his wound, the princess almost seemed disappointed. No. There wasn't any point in sharing her feelings with Miut.

Merib. Why did her stomach tighten at just the thought of him? As she stared into the pool, she thought she saw Merib's reflection staring back at her. She could faintly make out his high cheekbones and chiseled jaw line.

Amata felt a gentle touch on her shoulder.

"You seem lost in thought."

Amata jumped as she recognized Merib's voice. She actually *had* seen his reflection in the water. She turned to look at him. "It seems you always find me here lost in thought."

Merib sat next to her on the wall. "Care to share what's on your mind?"

Amata opened her mouth but then hesitated. How could she confide in Merib? He was a prince, heir to the throne of Egypt. Although she was the daughter of a Babylonian court healer, she was still a foreigner.

Merib gave her a half smile. "Tell you what. I'll go first. The last time you and I sat here, you challenged me to take action against Egyptian nomarchs who made unauthorized cutbacks in food allotments for the people in their cities. I'll have you know that I've discovered two nomarchs guilty of such mismanagement. They are now being held accountable for their misdeeds."

Amata's eyebrows rose. "Well done, Prince Merib. I know your people will appreciate that."

Merib's forehead suddenly furrowed. "However, I do hold you responsible for the attack on my life."

Amata drew in a quick breath and held up her hands. "No, Prince Merib. Surely you don't think I had anything to do with that!"

Merib grinned. "I'm only teasing. A little. I do think that your encouragement to take a more active role in the affairs of state did have something to do with my attempted assassination, but of course it wasn't your fault. In fact, I'm very grateful."

"For what?"

Merib brushed his fingers across Amata's hand. "For challenging me to take my position as the Prince of Egypt more seriously. I love my people, but I grew complacent with my role as Pharaoh's son. Princess Miut only thinks about wealth and increasing her power. I began to resent my royal status, disdaining our privileged position. You reminded me that I have a duty to the people of Egypt. Their welfare must be of paramount importance, even if I make enemies in the process."

Amata inhaled as she looked more deeply into Merib's dark-brown eyes. She noticed his eyes contained flecks of gold. She also knew that he hadn't removed his hand from hers. "I'm glad I could be of service."

"And now," Merib said, "I insist you tell me what's driven you into such deep thought that you didn't even notice my approach."

Amata shifted her gaze from Merib to the peach-colored lilies that gently waved in the breeze rippling across the pond. "It's my father. He spends all his time studying at the House of Scrolls. Learning about the disease that killed my mother seems more important to him than learning about his daughter. Sometimes I fear he's even forgotten my name."

Merib squeezed Amata's hand. "Have you told him how you feel?"

"No," she admitted. "We used to be close and talk about everything, but lately I feel so isolated and alone."

Merib still held her hand. "I often feel that way too. I hope you know you can always talk to me."

Amata looked at his hand that held hers and then up into his eyes once more. "And you with me. I mean, you can always talk with me too. If you want to. I know you're very busy." Amata's face grew warm.

"Prince Merib," a voice called out from the walkway. Amata saw a bodyguard approach. "The pharaoh requests your presence as he meets with the irrigation administrators," the bodyguard said.

Merib stood and nodded toward Amata. "Excuse me, Amata. Duty calls. I hope we can resume our discussion later."

Amata smiled. "Yes, I hope so too."

———————

Over the next three weeks, even though Merib's bodyguards were always nearby, Amata and Merib met almost every morning out at the pond. Amata told Merib about her growing love for the Egyptian people, their language, reverence for life, and spiritually seeking spirit. Merib confided that, in the future, Pharaoh planned to spend more time in Thebes, and he expected Merib to stay with him. She would miss her talks with Merib when she went back to Memphis.

"Are you sure you can't come back with us to Memphis?" Amata asked a few days before their planned return.

"My father expects me to remain with him in Thebes for a few more weeks," Merib explained. "He feels threatened by the Hyksos who have moved into northern Egypt from the area of Canaan, especially the nomadic Amorites, but also the Hurrians and the Hittites. My father will meet with his advisors here in Thebes to discuss the growing threat of the Hyksos. He wants me here during those discussions. I think he's afraid of these foreigners' growing influence, and so he's avoiding any confrontation with them."

Amata's eyes widened. "Does Pharaoh expect these foreigners will stage an uprising in Lower Egypt?"

"Possibly." Merib looked off across the pond. "All anyone thinks of these days is power and wealth. The priests and nomarchs want more power, and the foreigners want larger profits."

"And what do you want?"

Prince Merib studied Amata's face before he spoke. "I want what's best for Egypt."

Amata lost herself in Merib's eyes. Would she possibly play a part in what was best for Egypt?

———— • ————

Two days before Princess Miut and Amata returned to Memphis, Merib sent Amata a message to meet him again early the next morning. This time, he asked her to meet him in the vineyard beyond the pond.

As Amata waited for Merib among the grapevines, she drew in the sharp tangy fragrance of the ripe fruit. Merib came up from behind, offered her a grape, and popped it into her mouth.

"So delicious," she said around the grape.

Amata looked around for Merib's bodyguards, but saw none.

Merib anticipated her question. "They're watching, but I asked them to stay far enough away in order to give us some privacy. I have something to discuss that is for your ears only."

Amata bobbed on her toes. She would miss her chats with Merib when she went back to Memphis.

"Does what you want to tell me have anything to do with the Hyksos?" Amata grasped her hands in front of her and forced herself to stop bouncing and stand still.

"Yes, a little. I feel so comfortable talking with you about political matters. You help me sort things out. While I've been recuperating from my chest wound here in Thebes, my trusted advisers in Memphis report that the Hyksos' power in Lower Egypt continues to increase." Merib took Amata's hands and invited her to sit on the ground next to him before he continued.

"You see, previous pharaohs welcomed the Hyksos with open arms. They needed help with their extensive building projects, such as Amenemhat III's Great Canal. Other pharaohs had mining projects. The Hyksos proved able builders and craftsmen. After the works were completed, however, the Hyksos stayed and settled in Egypt instead of going home. And then there's the growing tribe of Hebrews who originally came here to escape a famine in Canaan. My father fears that these foreigners may eventually threaten his political power. Instead of taking a stand against them, however, he hides away here in Thebes."

Amata clutched at the weeds growing beneath the grapevines. An overthrow of Pharaoh would upset the balance of life for all Egyptians, people she was beginning to consider her own. "What will you do?"

"That's why I wanted to talk with you. My father believes it's time for me to marry. I suggested that marrying a woman of Semitic origin might strengthen my stand against the Hyksos. What do you think?"

Amata's heart picked up its beat. Was he referring to her? She was a Semite, but from Babylonia, not from Canaan. Surely he meant to marry a Semite from Canaan in order to strengthen ties with the Hyksos. "I think marrying a Canaanite could be very beneficial."

Merib reached out and grasped Amata's hands. "I suggested you."

Amata's heart beat faster. She felt blood pulsing in her ears. This couldn't be happening. She had to remain calm.

She squeezed Merib's hands and squeaked out her question. "And what did Pharaoh say?"

"He told me to arrange it."

Merib leaned in and kissed Amata's forehead.

"Well," Amata almost whispered. "Then, I think you should obey Pharaoh, don't you?"

Merib lifted Amata's chin and kissed her lips.

She didn't pull away.

—•—

Much happened over the next two days before Princess Miut and Amata returned to Memphis. Merib swore Amata to secrecy until he could arrange the details. Above all, he didn't want Princess Miut to get wind of the planned marriage. Amata agreed.

The day before Amata returned to Memphis, Merib caught up with her in the great hallway. The sun's early morning rays sent a shaft of light through a high window in the otherwise dim stone corridor. Bending down slightly, Merib whispered in Amata's ear. "I'll be going back to Memphis with you tomorrow after all. I need to move the wedding forward as quickly as possible."

Amata's stomach flipped and flopped with excitement, like a perch pulled from the Nile.

Merib watched several servants pass before he continued. "I also wanted to let you know that I'm going on a short hunting excursion this morning."

Now Amata's stomach lurched, as if the flopping perch had been speared. "Are you sure you've recovered enough from your injury?"

Merib looked around the hallway. No one stood within earshot. "Yes. And even if I'm not, I need to appear strong. Others watch me carefully, and word will get back to the delta region that the prince is not to be trifled with. This outing will prove that. Now, more than ever, I must appear as the strong leader Egypt needs for whatever lies ahead."

Amata lightly touched the place where the arrow had pierced Merib's chest. "You *are* the strong leader Egypt needs. I don't want you to go, but if you must, please be careful out there."

Just then Princess Miut walked down the hallway. Amata quickly removed her hand from Merib's chest.

"I heard about your hunting expedition, Prince Merib," Miut said. "Would you mind if Amata and I watched from a safe distance?"

"Not at all, Princess Miut." Merib bowed slightly. "I will have my bodyguards make the arrangements."

———

Later that morning Amata and Miut stood on a hill watching a herd of gazelle drink from the watering hole below. Before long, Amata saw Merib's hunting party approach. The dogs barked and howled. Frantic gazelles fled in all directions. Arrows whizzed through the air. Amata swelled with pride as she watched two of Merib's arrows hit their mark. Then the unthinkable happened. A stray arrow pierced Merib's chest. He fell to the ground, blood oozing from his wound.

The dogs continued to chase the gazelles, but the men in the hunting party converged on the prince, blocking her view. "No!" Amata screamed. She started to run down the hill, but a bodyguard stopped her.

"Let his men attend to him," the guard said.

Amata turned to Princess Miut. "How could this happen?" Amata wailed.

Princess Miut shook her head. "Accidents happen. There's nothing we can do right now. Let's return to the palace and wait for the physicians' report."

———

Amata stood in the Theban palace hallway numb and lightheaded, as if she'd just run up and down the staircase of a high tower. For the past two hours she'd stood outside Merib's chambers while physicians and priests tended his wound and incanted prayers. Now soldiers carried the limp body of Prince Merib past her as the queen wailed and brushed hair from her dead son's eyes.

Princess Miut grabbed one of the soldier's arms and followed along beside them. "Do we know who is responsible for this?" The princess screamed.

"It was an accident," the soldier replied. "A stray arrow pierced his chest near the heart. The physicians could not stop the bleeding."

"Who shot the arrow?" the princess demanded. "He must be punished!"

"We don't know." The soldier near Merib's head readjusted his grip. Amata stood frozen in place. She blinked hard and fast. Her body began to tremble and she sucked in air that refused to fill her lungs. Her mind raced. She asked him not to go. This looked like the work of an assassin, but there was no way to prove it. What would happen to Egypt now?

TWELVE

Sam grumbled under his breath. Amata returned from her latest trip to Thebes over a week ago, but she hadn't spoken a word to him or Balashi since she'd returned. She rarely came out of her room except to eat. Eshe hadn't been over for the last two days because she had a high fever and remained at her own home, cared for by her family. Now, this morning, Balashi woke with a fever. Sam dipped another cloth into a bowl of cool water, twisted out the excess liquid, and placed it on Balashi's forehead. Whatever was ailing Amata, she needed to get over it. At least she could go to the market and get some food. Sam dried his hands and walked to her room.

He saw Amata sitting on her bed, lightly fingering Uru's alabaster jar. Tears ran down her cheeks. The sight melted Sam's anger.

"You haven't said a word since you returned from Thebes," he began. "I know Prince Merib had a hunting accident, but I don't know why you . . ." Sam couldn't finish his sentence. He sat next to her on her bed, searching for the right words.

Amata's eyes never left the small jar in her hands. "He asked me to marry him."

Her voice sounded weak and far away. "Marry who? Uru?"

Amata turned to face Sam. She wiped her cheeks with the back of her hand. "Merib. He asked me to marry him before he was . . . Oh, Sam!" Sobs choked out the rest of her words. Amata put down the jar and threw her arms around Sam's neck.

Sam's heart felt too big for his chest. He awkwardly rubbed Amata's back and let her cry. "I'm sorry. I didn't even know you and Merib were close." Sam shook his head. *Merib asked Amata to marry him?* Those words, strung together, sounded as though she had delivered them in an incomprehensible language. He couldn't absorb the thought.

Just then Balashi weakly called from his room. "Sam. Water, please."

Amata let go of Sam and held him at arm's length. "Is Father sick?"

"He has a fever, just like Eshe." Sam rose and went to Balashi. Amata would've known about Balashi's illness if she had bothered to come out of her room. Sam bit his tongue to keep the caustic words from coming out. He then felt a stab in his chest. Here Amata had been in her room all week and she never said a word about her grief over Merib's death. Had the three of them grown so far apart that they could no longer share in each other's pain?

As Sam entered Balashi's bedchamber, he heard the front door open and then shut. Sam's jaw clenched. How could she just leave him alone to take care of their father? Sam raised Balashi's head and pressed a cup of water to his dry lips.

Sam sat in a chair next to Balashi's bed and continued to put cool compresses on his adoptive father's head. He dozed off until Amata returned a while later. He heard her speak with someone as she entered the house. Who had come back with her? Then he recognized the voice. She'd returned with Qar!

"My friend," the Chief Physician greeted Balashi as he entered the bedroom. "I see you have succumbed to the illness that has recently afflicted so many here in Memphis."

Balashi reached out his wrinkled hand and grasped Qar's brown-spotted arm. "Qar. You didn't need to come. It's just a fever. It should pass soon."

Sam shook his head. Balashi's voice sounded weaker than it had earlier that morning. Sam turned and saw

Amata framing the doorway with her alabaster jar clutched to her chest.

"Thank you," Sam mouthed to her.

Qar withdrew willow leaves from his medicine bag. "Sam, make a tea with these, please."

Sam threw back his head. Of course. Why hadn't he thought of that? Willow bark and leaves for fevers. He and Balashi used them all the time in Babylon.

Amata entered the room and placed her alabaster jar on a wicker chest near Balashi's bed. "What can I do?"

Qar handed her a small pouch. "Take these coriander seeds, add water, and make a paste."

Sam paused before leaving to make the tea. "What's the coriander paste for?"

"His aching joints," Qar responded.

Balashi tried to lift his head. "How did you know my joints ached?"

Qar smiled. "I *am* the Chief Physician, am I not?"

After drinking his tea and receiving a coriander rub, the tightness in Balashi's face slackened. His eyes closed and he drew in a deep breath.

Qar felt his friend's forehead. "Much better. Rest now. I will look in on you after a while."

Amata picked up her jar from the chest where she left it, and walked out with Sam and Qar.

"May I see that?" Qar asked as they moved to the common living area.

Amata handed the alabaster jar to Qar.

The physician turned it over in his hands, tracing the swirling bands of cream and brown. "This looks very old. Where did you get it?"

Sam saw Amata blush. "A good friend gave it to me."

Qar looked at the bottom of the jar and pointed to the hieroglyphs engraved there. "Notice how these glyphs appear taut and slender. This is in keeping with the style of writing used around the time of the early pharaohs. I do hope your friend bought this alabaster jar from a reputable source. I would hate to think it was stolen from an ancient tomb." Qar quietly handed the jar back to Amata.

Qar then placed a hand on Sam's shoulder. "Why don't you two go to the Delta to purchase some fish, fruit and vegetables? I hear Eshe has not been here in several days, and I'm sure you could both use some fresh air. I will stay here and watch over your father while you are gone."

———————

By the time Sam and Amata reached the Delta, the smell of freshly cooked onions, garlic and fish made Sam's mouth water. The growl in his stomach reprimanded him for missing his morning meal. The sun now stood directly overhead. Sam used Balashi's bull seal to purchase two cooked fish wrapped in palm leaves, and gave one of the packets to Amata. As they walked over to the fruit and vegetable stalls, Sam noticed Amata gently leading him in the direction of the pier.

Sam took his last bite of fish and then stated the obvious. "Before we see if Uru's ship has docked, aren't you even curious to know if I've gone back to the hidden tomb?"

Amata stopped and tugged on the sleeve of Sam's tunic. "You always seem to know what I plan to do—sometimes even before I do. Yes, I'd like to go to the docks to see if Uru's ship has come back yet. And yes, I'm sorry I've ignored you all week. I do want to hear about the tomb. It's just that I . . ."

Sam saw water begin to pool in Amata's eyes. Wishing to save her the struggle of an overflow, he quickly jumped in. "The tomb now has a secret panel. It looks like someone's storing grain there."

Amata's eyes widened. "Merib and I were just talking about that last week before he . . ."

Again Sam jumped in. "You and Merib were talking about secret panels?"

Amata rolled her eyes. "No, silly. We were talking about nomarchs keeping grain from the people under their care. Maybe the nomarch of Memphis is storing extra grain in the hidden tomb so he can sell it for his own profit."

Amata's words came out with more energy than anything she'd said in the last several weeks. If he could keep her interested in solving the mystery of the hidden tomb, maybe it would ease some of the pain she felt over Merib's death. He decided not to tell her just yet about his suspicions that Keret created the tomb's secret panel.

"Amata!" a voice rang out from the direction of the pier. Sam and Amata turned to see a bearded young sailor approach them.

"Uru." Amata cried out. "It's so good to see you."

Uru's arms opened wide as if to embrace Amata, but stopped midair when he saw Sam. Instead, he clapped his hands over his head. "And you! I'm sorry I've been gone so long. We had bad weather on the return trip."

Amata smiled. "Uru, I'd like to introduce to you my brother, Samsuluna."

The two young men nodded their heads in acknowledgement.

"Samsuluna," Uru nodded again, "Amata's told me much about you."

Sam noticed that Uru's brown eyes twinkled as he smiled. Even though he felt protective of Amata and wished she didn't have any interest in young men, he couldn't help but like Uru instantly.

Uru tapped Sam's shoulder. "Come. I will show you my ship."

Uru introduced Sam to his cousin, Barak, who showed Sam the boat's rigging, the waterproofed location for their provisions during voyages, and how they stored goods purchased for trade. All the while, Sam kept Uru and Amata in view as they talked, smiled, laughed, and eventually cried together. The scene made Sam's throat burn with a bittersweet taste. Then a warm sensation flooded him. It was like his first sip of wine. Yes, perhaps he could share his sister's friendship with a young man like Uru.

Barak smacked the top of a tall clay jar as he completed their tour. "And now that these are empty, we will fill them once again with Egyptian goods, stamp them with our seal, and sell their contents at Mediterranean ports."

Sam looked at the top of the clay jar. Part of the broken seal still remained, and it looked familiar. "What do you use for your seal?"

Barak held up the blue-green ceramic seal that hung around his neck. "We use a seal in the shape of a scarab beetle with a bull inscribed on it." Barak moved the seal closer for Sam to see. "The bull represents our chief Canaanite god, Baal. Since the scarab is important to the Egyptians, we thought we'd combine the two symbols to create our own unique seal."

Was it the constant rocking of the boat that made Sam's stomach suddenly feel as though he had to retch? No. The scarab-shaped bull seal around Barak's neck looked exactly like the seal he'd seen on the jars in the hidden tomb. He didn't know what the connection was, but Uru and Barak were somehow linked to grain hidden in the tomb. He glanced once more at Amata. She looked so happy talking with Uru, but he had to protect her. He had to find out the truth.

THIRTEEN

Over the next several days, Sam and Amata took turns giving Balashi sips of willow bark tea, coriander paste rubs, and cool compresses to bring down his fever. One afternoon while giving Balashi some tea, Sam heard someone knocking on the front door.

"I'll see who's here," Amata said.

Sam hoped Eshe had returned. As much as he appreciated Amata's attempts at cooking, he didn't think he could take another meal of burnt fish or chew another bite of her coarse bread.

Amata entered her father's bedchamber just as Sam laid another cool cloth on Balashi's forehead.

Amata placed a tray of bread and vegetables on Balashi's nightstand and then gently stroked her father's hair. Glancing back at the vegetable tray, she smiled at Sam. "I thought I'd give you a meal that I couldn't burn." Turning once again to her father she asked Sam, "Has he been sleeping all morning?"

Sam reached over to the vegetable tray and, passing over the bread, picked up a piece of celery and a radish. "Yes, but I'm afraid that even in his sleep, Father's not getting the rest he needs. He's tossed and turned all morning. He moans in his sleep and says things I can only partially understand." Sam crunched on a stalk of celery and then asked, "Who was at the door just now?"

"Oh, I'm sorry." Before she answered Sam, she removed the cloth from her father's head, dipped it in the cool water, wrung it out and placed it once again on his head. "It was Eshe's oldest son. He said Eshe's recovered from her fever, but she's now busy caring for her husband and their youngest son. It will be several more days before she can return to help us here."

Sam groaned, a little more forcefully than he intended. He saw a look of hurt flash across Amata's face. "Well, I'm sure we can manage without Eshe for a few more days," he quickly added. "We haven't starved yet!" Sam took a cucumber from the tray and bit into it.

Amata laughed. "No, we haven't starved yet, but I should go to the market again. I planned to go this morning, but I didn't sleep much last night when it was my turn to watch Father. Like you said, he talks a lot in his sleep."

Suddenly, without opening his eyes, Balashi cried out. "No, Amata, please don't go. I'm so sorry. It's all my fault." Balashi then mumbled something incomprehensible.

Amata took a step back and held a hand to her mouth. "Sam, is Father awake or asleep? Do you think he heard me talk about going to the market? Does he not want me to go?"

Sam shook his head. "I'm sure he's still asleep. He's said things like that all morning. I'm not sure what he's talking about."

Balashi's head turned from side to side, but he continued to sleep. Amata put her face in her hands and collapsed to the floor. "I've been so cruel to Father the past few months." She began to cry. "What if he never wakes up? I'll never get a chance to apologize." Her soft sobs shook her body.

Sam removed the cloth from Balashi's forehead and twisted it in his hands. He had tried so hard to keep his new family together. The thought of losing Balashi stopped his breath.

Amata looked up at Sam. "I've stayed away from you and Father the past two months because I thought you didn't want me around. You both seemed so happy and so busy with your studies here. I guess I felt left out and lost. That's why I began to spend so much time with Princess Miut. At first it seemed like she wanted me around. She made me feel special, almost like a sister."

"And now?" Sam continued to twist the cloth.

"Even when I thought she was my friend, I still felt lost and alone. Then, when Prince Merib and I started spending time together, she began to ignore me. Now with Merib gone, I don't want to ever go back to the palace. And yet, that makes me feel even more lost."

Sam felt a burning in his chest that slowly inched its way to his throat. "I'm so sorry, Amata," Sam choked out. "I had no idea you felt that way. It makes my heart hurt to hear you say those things."

"It's not your fault, Sam. I pushed both you and Father away. I felt angry and didn't know how to deal with it. I've always seen myself as the daughter of Babylonia's Great *Asu*. Later I also saw myself as Samsuluna's sister. Here in Egypt, with you and Father away so much, I wasn't sure who I was any more." Amata rubbed her wet cheeks with the back of her hand. "And Sam, there's something else."

Sam looked at Balashi. He appeared calm once again. He looked back at Amata. "What is it?"

"I don't think Merib's death was an accident."

Just then Sam heard the wooden sound of knocking again. He handed Amata the cloth and went to see who had come.

"Keret!" Sam shouted when he found his friend at the doorway. "Come in!"

Keret entered the reception room, accompanied by a young man Sam recognized as one of Keret's paid servants. Keret handed Sam a bundled package. "Qar stopped by the shop this morning and told us about Balashi. He also said that Eshe has been ill. I have two helpers at home, so Anut here agreed to come and cook for you as long as you need him."

Sam looked down at the package Keret gave him. "I don't know what to say." Sam bowed. "Thanks to both of you for your gracious offer."

Anut pointed to the bundle in Sam's hands. "That package contains food for the next few meals. I will also clean and do whatever else you need done while Eshe is away."

"Did I hear something about meals?" Amata said as she came out of Balashi's bedroom.

Keret laughed. "Yes, but don't get too fond of Anut's cooking. He's the best cook I've ever had, and he's only on loan for a short while. I do expect him back when Balashi recovers."

Sam handed the bundle to Anut. "Could you make us a big loaf of bread for dinner? Amata can show you the cooking area."

Anut took the package and bowed. "I will make you a meal of bread, lentil soup, and vegetables for this evening. Keret even sent along some lamb we can have tonight and then I will make lamb stew tomorrow."

Sam's mouth began to water. He couldn't remember the last time he ate lamb.

"And I imagine you've taken turns watching Balashi every night," Anut added. "If you would like, I will sit with him this evening so that you can both get your rest. Once your father gets well, it would be a shame for either of you to come down with this illness because you became weak while caring for him."

Sam sighed. "That sounds like a wonderful idea. I don't think I've slept well for the past three nights."

Amata led Anut to the cooking area and Keret turned to leave.

"Wait," Sam called out. "How are you doing, Keret? We haven't talked much since Fenuku's death."

Keret stopped and turned to face Sam, but looked down at the floor.

Sam pressed on. "In fact, the last time we talked, you said nothing was going the way you'd planned, but that you were going to fix that. Are things going any better for you now?"

Keret didn't look up at Sam. "I appreciate your friendship Sam, but I'd rather not talk about it right now. I have some things to think through."

Sam chewed a corner of his lower lip. He knew there was something Keret wasn't telling him.

Sam held up a hand. "I'm sorry. I respect your privacy, Keret. It's just that I've missed your friendship this past month. Amata, as you may know, spends most of her free time with Princess Miut and her family, while Balashi and I spend most of our time studying and visiting patients. I miss spending time with people my own age."

Keret nodded. "So do I Sam. When Balashi's better, why don't you and Amata stop by the shop again? I've been working extra hard and should be able to take time off soon. Perhaps the three of us can go sailing on the Delta. I have a friend who will lend us his boat."

"I know Amata would love that, and so would I." Sam wanted to tell Keret that he'd seen him with Princess Miut in the palace, but felt embarrassed. He also wanted to ask about the secret panel in the tomb but feared Keret would say he didn't know anything about it. In Babylon, Sam never had close friends except for Enlil, and he wasn't sure how to proceed.

Finally, Sam decided to test the waters. "And when Balashi is better, Amata and I were also going to explore that hidden tomb near Giza I told you about. Would you like to explore that with us?" Sam held his breath, wondering how Keret would respond.

Keret's brows scrunched together. His face darkened. "Sam, don't go near any tomb in Giza. The ground there is very unstable. You could get buried alive if a tomb caved in. Promise me you'll stay away from there."

Sam bit back his thought. *I will, if you will.* Now he felt sure Keret was hiding something. If the tombs around Giza really were unstable, why did Keret build the secret panel in the hidden tomb? Weren't friends supposed to trust each other? How could he trust Keret if he didn't tell him the truth? Sam vowed to get to the bottom of the mystery and find out how Keret, Nakthor, Uru and Barak were involved.

FOURTEEN

Sam glanced up from his dinner of quail to look at Balashi sitting across from him and at Amata on his left. "This is nice, eating together again," he said.

Two weeks had passed since Balashi recovered from his illness, and since then they'd eaten every morning and evening meal together.

"Yes, it is," Amata agreed. "I've missed this. And I'm certainly glad Eshe was able to come back last week. I didn't know that cooking for three people could be so difficult."

Sam poked her in the arm. "You think cooking was hard? Eating it was even harder!"

Amata winced in mock pain, and then laughed. "Well, from now on, Eshe's agreed to give me cooking lessons at least once a week. I'm sure to get better over time."

Sam swallowed his last bite of Eshe's meal and then rubbed his stomach. Things seemed to have returned to normal. And now that he and Balashi weren't so busy helping people recover from the recent epidemic, he decided to ask Balashi for a day off. Just as he opened his mouth, Balashi spoke.

Balashi leaned toward his daughter. "Amata, I notice you haven't made any visits to the palace the past few weeks. Is everything all right?"

Sam knew Amata hadn't told Balashi about her secret engagement to Merib. All Balashi knew was that Merib died in a hunting accident three weeks ago. Sam's full stomach tightened into a knot. He wished Amata would just tell Balashi everything.

Amata slowly sipped her drink before she answered her father. "I hear that Pharaoh and his Great Wife have remained in Thebes since Prince Merib died. As their only son, Merib's loss came as quite a blow. Pharaoh's other wives and children have all remained here in Memphis since the—accident, including Princess Miut, but she and I have somewhat drifted apart."

Sam noticed how Amata paused before she said the word "accident."

Balashi slowly stroked his beard. "Well, I have an apology to make, Amata. Since my illness, I've come to realize that I may have pushed you away. That was not my intent. I'm sorry. Since our move to Egypt, I've spent too much time and energy trying to find a cure for the disease that claimed your mother's life."

Balashi's voice grew thick. "Ever since her death, I felt that I had failed your mother as a husband and as an *asu*."

Amata broke in. "No, Father, you . . ."

Balashi held up a hand and continued. "I thought that if I found the cure, perhaps I could redeem myself. In the process, my pride almost cost me what I value most—my family. I want you and Sam to know that you both mean more to me than life itself. I'm just sorry that it took a grave illness for me to figure that out."

Amata rose from her cushion and embraced her father. "I love you Father. And I'm sorry I also pushed you away and did things against your wishes. I just felt so lost."

Sam breathed a sigh of relief. Perhaps things would now return to normal.

———————

The next morning, having received Balashi's permission to take a day off, Sam and Amata rode a donkey to the port at Peru-Nefer. They hoped to take Keret up on his promise of a boat ride in the Delta, and then visit the hidden tomb. As they walked into the shop, they saw Keret standing at his worktable with a sheet of papyrus stretched out before him. Finely-ruled small squares filled the page. Spread across the grid Sam saw a drawing that looked like a hunting scene. Sam watched as Keret studied the grid-filled image and then made small marks with a writing tool.

Amata leaned in closer for a better look. Suddenly she gasped and put a hand to her mouth.

Sam also took a closer look. He saw what looked like Prince Merib and his men hunting gazelles. Dogs barked around the men's heels as arrows whizzed through the air.

Keret looked up at Sam and Amata, and then back at the sketch. "I'm sorry, Sam. I'm very busy right now. I can't talk."

"No time for that boat ride on the Delta, huh?"

Keret shook his head from side to side without looking up. "Not now, or in the foreseeable future. The Master Sculptor told me to review these sketches for wall panels. Tomorrow I start sculpting this scene on a panel in Prince Merib's tomb at the royal necropolis in Dashur."

Amata moaned, then turned and ran out of the shop.

"You should go after her, Sam." Keret spoke without looking up.

"Not before I ask you a question." Sam widened his stance, as if to brace himself. "You warned me not to explore any hidden tombs in Giza because the tombs might cave in. Is that the real reason?"

Before Keret answered, Nakthor entered the shop. The priest eyed Sam up and down. "What are you doing here, Foreigner?" Nakthor shouted in his high-pitched voice. "Leave at once. This sculptor is working on important royal business, and I'll not have you getting in his way."

The priest then turned to Keret. "I am to marry Princess Miut in two weeks," he announced. "When you finish the panel for Prince Merib's tomb, you must immediately begin sculpting a statue of me sitting next to Princess Miut. I have already discussed this project with the Master Sculptor. He will give you the details."

Nakthor turned and looked at Sam again. "Are you still here, Foreigner? Be gone!" Nakthor waved the back of his hand at Sam, as if to shoo him out the door.

Sam turned to go, but not before hearing Nakthor tell Keret, "And we are having trouble with one of your doors. I will send someone when we are ready for you to come and repair it."

Sam found Amata down by the docks near Uru's ship. Uru's men scurried around the deck and riggings, but Uru and Barak were nowhere in sight.

Sam quietly approached Amata. "Looking for Uru?"

Amata turned and looked up at Sam with moist eyes. "Just when I feel as though my heart has begun to heal, something reminds me of Merib and I feel like it's torn in two again."

One of Uru's bearded crewmembers walked down the ship's gangplank and called out to Amata. "If you're looking for Uru, he went off in search of Barak. We depart for Phoenicia again in two days, and Barak was supposed to be here this morning with the final loads of grain."

"Poor Uru," Amata said to Sam. "He told me that Barak has grown more and more irresponsible the past few months. It's Uru's job to sell the items they bring here from other countries. It's Barak's job to buy goods from the Egyptians that they then sell abroad. Barak's supposed to barter with the Egyptians for the best grain prices so they can make a good profit when they sell the grain to merchants in Canaan. Lately, Uru's had to do both the buying and the selling."

Sam laid a hand on Amata's shoulder. "Well, since we can't go boating on the Delta today, and you can't find Uru, why don't we go and explore the hidden tomb?"

FIFTEEN

Two hours later, Sam and Amata reached the Giza plateau.

"Why did we stop so far away from the hidden tomb?" Amata asked.

Sam stopped near a clump of palm trees about forty rods from the sand dune that disguised the tomb's entrance and slid off the donkey. "I'm not sure how long we'll be inside," he said. "I don't want the presence of our jenny near the tomb to let anyone know we're inside." Sam patted the animal's rear end. "Besides, she'll have shade here while we're gone."

Sam saw Amata's eyes narrow as he helped her down.

"Sam, this isn't going to be dangerous, is it?"

Sam tethered the donkey to one of the palm trees. "Of course not." He smiled. "We're just out for a little exploration."

Sam removed the skin of water he'd tied to the donkey's saddle and handed it to Amata. He also removed a leather pack and mentally reviewed its contents: a rope, a clay container of hot coals, a jug of oil, an oil lamp, and a package of dried figs. After shouldering the pack, he patted his side to make sure he had his bronze dagger under his tunic. He then grabbed his walking stick and headed out with Amata for the tomb's entrance.

Fifteen minutes later, they found the boulder that covered the tomb's opening. After walking through the short tunnel, they reached the first room. Sam filled the oil lamp and lit it. Its glow cast eerie shadows around the small enclosure. Sam showed Amata the hieroglyphs of prayers and painted pictures of the gods that decorated the otherwise empty room.

Sam carried the lamp to the back wall and found the crack he'd seen on his last visit. "Watch this," he told Amata.

Sam pulled on one of the torch brackets that lined the wall. Nothing happened. Sam pulled on three more brackets, but again, nothing. "The last time I pulled on these, this wall opened up," Sam explained.

Then he remembered Nakthor's words to Keret before he left the shop. "We're having trouble with one of your doors."

Perhaps this was the door Nakthor was talking about.

Amata followed the wall to where it met the adjacent wall. "Sam, look at this," she called out.

Sam walked over and held the lamp toward the area where Amata pointed. Someone had punched an opening in the wall near the floor, just large enough to crawl through.

Amata bent down and peered inside. "Maybe when they couldn't open the secret panel they knocked a hole in this wall and tried to get in through here."

"It's worth a look," Sam said. He handed the oil lamp to Amata and crawled through. Amata then bent down and handed the lamp back to Sam so she could crawl through.

With both of them inside, Sam held up the lamp as high as possible. The second room appeared larger than the first, but it wasn't the room behind the panel that had contained the jars of wheat. At the far end of the chamber, Sam saw what looked like a wooden sarcophagus. Nearby lay a wooden statue of Anubis, the jackal, posed in a sitting position. It now laid on its side. As Sam and Amata stepped closer to the statue of Anubis, they saw a colorful canopic chest. The sides were decorated with colorful images of Osiris, Anubis, Thoth and Horus. A broken side of the chest revealed its contents, four canopic jars. Sam knew that the jars preserved someone's stomach, intestines, liver, and lungs. To his

left Sam saw another broken chest, this one full of shabtis. They looked like miniature mummies and carried baskets of farming tools.

Amata, on Sam's right, took a few steps away from him. "Can you shine the light over here, Sam?" she asked.

Just as Sam turned, Amata screamed.

Sam stepped forward with the lamp and then lost his footing.

"Ahh!" Sam yelled as he plunged into darkness.

Sam heard his clay lamp crash to the floor at the same moment he hit the bottom. Sam sat in the dark for a few seconds, trying to make sense of what happened. "Amata. Where are you? Are you all right?"

Amata moaned. "I fell into a hole or something, and hit my head."

Sam heard what sounded like small pebbles scraping against the slate floor. It sounded like Amata was moving around somewhere nearby, but he couldn't see a thing.

"Ow," Amata shouted. "I think I also hurt my ankle when I fell. Where are we?"

Sam sat up and felt the surrounding area. Near his feet he touched something moist. Rubbing his fingers together, he brought his hand to his nose. The smell reminded him of the hair treatment he'd made last week for Iny's wife. She asked for something to help her hair grow, so Sam made a paste that included castor oil. Sam had also used castor oil in his lamp. It must have spilled out when it crashed to the floor. Sam also noticed that the hem of his tunic felt damp. Sam pushed himself up and tried to stand, but a sharp pain shot through his left wrist.

Sam reached out again into the surrounding blackness. "Amata, see if you can find our pack. If we can light a torch with our coals, we can see where we are."

"Wait, Sam," Amata whispered from nearby. "I think I hear voices."

Sam sat very still. He heard the tink of a stone hammer hitting rock, then the sound of falling stones.

"When I couldn't get the sculptor's panel open to get our wheat out, I tried going through this wall here," a deep voice said above the sounds of the hammer. "I squeezed through this small hole, but I think we need to make it bigger in order to take things out."

"And you say you found a new treasure room?" a second voice asked. "Are you sure the priest doesn't know anything about it?"

"I'm sure, Palti," the deeper voice answered. "I knew I'd need help getting everything out, so I came back for you."

Sam felt Amata grab his arm. "I know that deep voice," she whispered. "It sounds like Barak, Uru's cousin."

"There. That should be big enough to get things out," the voice they now knew as Barak said. They heard the two men enter the room.

Sam saw a faint light reflect off the walls above them.

"Wow, look at all of this," Palti said. "You should be able to pay off all your debts with this treasure trove."

The light drew closer to Sam and Amata's hole.

"And what's down there?" Palti asked.

"Watch out!" Barak yelled. "The ground here gave way. If you fall in, you might break a leg. The sculptor said the tombs out here were easier to dig than the later tombs farther south. The ground here is made of slate and clay. Further south it's limestone. The ground here is easier to dig up, but it also gives way. That's what made this pit here."

Light from above lit up some of the objects in the hole. Sam motioned for Amata to join him behind a canopic chest where he hoped Barak and Palti wouldn't see them.

"So that's why you had me bring a rope," Palti said.

"Well, I sure didn't bring you because of your brains." Barak laughed. "Let's collect the treasures from up here first. Then I'll lower you down and you can get things from below."

The light seemed to move further away from the pit.

"Isn't Nakthor supposed to be here soon with the sculptor?" Palti asked.

"He won't get here until after midday," Barak replied. "That will give us enough time to grab the most valuable treasures before that snooty priest sees we've taken them. Then you'll load them onto our donkey and stow them away on our ship. We'll split the profit after we sell them to merchants in Phoenicia, just like I promised, and my cousin won't be any the wiser."

"There should be enough here to pay off all your gambling debts—both here and in Phoenicia."

Sam felt Amata's grip on his arm. "Sam, what are we going to do? If they come down here, they'll find us for sure."

Sam reached for his dagger, but thought better of it. He knew they'd be no match for the two men.

Just then the sound of distant voices drifted in.

"Quick, Palti, take these bags and wait in here. It sounds like Nakthor and the sculptor got here early. Once we get the panel fixed and I go into the larger room with the priest, take what you can grab and get back to the ship. I'll meet you later."

Sam heard a familiar high-pitched voice. "So, can you fix it quickly, or will we have to come back?"

Nakthor had arrived.

"I'll see what I can do."

Sam recognized the other voice as Keret's.

"What's Keret doing here?" Amata whispered to Sam.

Sam squeezed his arm just above his injured wrist to lessen the pulsing pain. He should have told Amata earlier about the secret panel in Princess Miut's room, and his suspicion that Keret made the panel in the hidden tomb. Sam shook his head as he began to fit the pieces together. After Nakthor caught Keret in Princess Miut's bedroom chambers, the priest probably blackmailed Keret into working for him, but he couldn't explain any of that to Amata right now—not with Palti right above them.

A chill spread throughout Sam's body. "Shhh," was all he managed to say.

Sam and Amata sat in the dark and waited. Eventually they heard a loud grunt and the grinding of stone against stone.

"It should work fine now," Keret said. "But remember, I warned you about the ground being unstable. They stopped making tombs out here a long time ago for a reason. If the clay and slate layers underneath give way, I can't guarantee your safety."

"Let me worry about that," Nakthor replied. "Your work here is done. Go now."

Muffled sounds and indistinct voices continued to echo through the chambers. Before long, Sam heard movement in the room above. He guessed Palti was grabbing a few more treasures before he headed back to Uru's ship.

When he was sure Palti had left, Sam whispered to Amata. "We need to get out of here before anyone finds us."

"But how?" Amata squeaked out.

"I have a plan, but we'll have to wait until Nakthor and Barak leave."

After about an hour, Sam heard the sound of stone sliding against stone once more. He guessed Nakthor and Barak had closed the secret panel.

"You and your workers will meet me here again tomorrow for our final transaction." Sam recognized Nakthor's voice once more. "I will bring the sculptor along just in case there is any further trouble with the door. Iny and his men will bring the last loads of grain from the Memphis nomarch. Bring your jars and men to take the grain to your ship. And be sure you bring our agreed upon payment. Otherwise, you and your cousin will never sail again."

The sound of small stones crunching under men's feet eventually faded. When all seemed quiet, Sam took out his dagger and began to cut off the hem of his tunic, but the slightest movement of his wrist caused stabbing pain. He bit his lip to keep himself from crying out.

"What are you doing?" Amata asked.

Sam continued to cut and tear, trying not to twist his left wrist. "The bottom of my tunic soaked up some of the oil that spilled." Sam felt around the space near him, but in the dark, he couldn't even see his hand in front of his face.

"Feel around for our pack," Sam said.

Sam heard Amata moving. "Here, I found it," she called out.

"Ouch!" Sam yelled as Amata smacked him with the pack. "That was my head, not my hand."

"Sorry. It's so dark. But it serves you right for getting us into this."

Sam rubbed the side of his head. "Well, now I'm going to get us out. Okay?"

Sam reached into the pack and found the jar with the coals. The jar had broken, but the coals still felt warm. Sam wrapped the oil-soaked hem around his knife's blade and then held the covered blade against one of the coals. Eventually, the oiled rag ignited. When he held the torch above his head, he saw that the hole was too deep to climb out, even if they stood on one of the broken chests and on each other's shoulders. He'd have to find another way to climb out.

Sam handed Amata the torch and then dragged the broken chest to the wall. Next, he broke off pieces of wood from the chest into short, narrow sticks and stuffed them into his tunic's belt. After picking up a fist-sized rock, he climbed onto the chest. "Can you get the rope out of the pack and hand it to me?" he asked Amata.

Amata found the coiled rope and handed it to Sam. "What do you plan to do?" she asked.

Sam shouldered the rope and smiled. "Watch." Sam used the rock to pound one of the short sticks into the clay wall just above his head. Then, using the stick as a foothold, he pounded another stick into the wall higher up.

Eventually Sam called down to Amata. "I'm almost there. When I get to the top, I'll drop the end of the rope down to you. Tie it around your waist and climb up. If you slip, I'll be hanging on to the other end until you get your footing again."

"Sam, I'm scared. I don't know if I can do it. My ankle's really sore."

"It'll be fine." Sam hoped he sounded confident, but his hands trembled and his left wrist throbbed. When he stepped onto his highest foothold, his fingers reached up and felt the flat surface of the top. He took in a deep breath and pulled out another stick. Just as he brought back his arm to pound with the rock, the stick under his left foot snapped. He clawed to find a hold, but his fingernails only gathered loose dirt and stones. He toppled backwards, hitting his head on something as he fell.

"Sam!" Amata screamed.

It was the last thing he heard before darkness enveloped him.

SIXTEEN

When Sam awoke, his head throbbed. He touched the back of his head and discovered an egg-sized lump. At least there wasn't any blood. His wrist, however, felt twice its size.

"Amata, where are you?" he called out. His throat felt raw.

"Sam." Amata sighed. "I'm so glad you're awake. You were out for quite a while." Amata's voice quivered. "I'm cold and I'm scared."

Sam tried to move. Every muscle ached. "How long was I out?"

"Well, if I could see the sun, I might be able to tell you." Amata's voice rose in pitch. "How do I know? A really long time. I got hungry and ate the dried figs, but I did manage to save you a few."

Sam heard Amata move across the slate floor. "Keep talking Sam, so I can find you."

"I'm so sorry I got us into this, Amata." Sam cleared his throat. It hurt to talk. He managed to get into a sitting position.

"There you are," Amata said, reaching out and touching his knee. "Sounds like you need some water."

She touched the skin of water to his knee and he gratefully reached for it, opened the stopper and swallowed a few sips.

After pushing the stopper back into place, Sam bumped Amata's arm with it. "Here, you hold it. How's your ankle doing?"

"I'll live. At least today. Nakthor said they'd be back tomorrow. Do you think we can get out of here before then, or will we have to let them find us when they come?"

"Right now I don't feel strong enough to try and climb the wall again. And with your ankle, I don't think you are either. Judging by my stomach, it feels like it's after dinner. Maybe we should just get some rest and see what happens in the morning."

"Sam, if we judge time by your stomach, it might only be after lunch." Amata managed to laugh. "You're always hungry."

Sam smiled, appreciating Amata's attempt to lighten the mood. Their hopes for a safe rescue, however, looked bleak. He knew if they couldn't get out of the pit by themselves, they'd have to call on Nakthor and Barak when they returned. Sam shuddered to think what those two might do when they found out their secret had been discovered.

Sam didn't voice his thoughts to Amata. "Let's just rest awhile." Sam closed his eyes and quickly fell asleep.

Sam awoke to the sound of someone calling his name, and decided he was dreaming. It sounded like Balashi's voice in the distance. "Samsuluna, Amata. Where are you?"

Sam heard Amata moving nearby. Then he felt a hand shaking his knee.

"Sam, Father's here! Sam, wake up!"

He wasn't dreaming. Somewhere above them, Balashi called out again. "Sam, Amata. Are you here?"

"Sam. Call out if you can hear us." This time the voice sounded like Keret's.

"Down here!" Sam shouted. "We're down here in a pit."

Amata joined in the shouting.

A few minutes later, Sam saw lights flicker above him.

"Be careful of the big hole," Sam shouted. "We fell in, and we can't get out."

Sam looked up and saw Balashi's shadowed face peer over the edge.

Amata stood and raised her arms. "Father! How did you find us? I'm so glad you're here."

"When you didn't return last night, I went to Keret's to ask about you," Balashi said. "Keret told me you had probably come here, so we set out this morning to find you."

In the torchlight from above, Sam saw Keret drop down the end of a rope.

"Tie the rope around Amata, and I'll pull her up," Keret told Sam. "We've got to pull both of you out quickly. Nakthor, Iny and Barak will be here soon. They won't be happy to know their secret's been discovered."

"And just what *is* going on?" Amata asked. "And how and why are you involved in all of this?"

Sam tied the rope around Amata and tested it to make sure it would hold.

"There'll be time to explain later," Keret said. "Right now, let's just get you out of here."

Sam pointed to the footholds on the wall. "Use those to help you up, but don't put pressure on your left ankle." Even in the dim torchlight, Sam saw that Amata's ankle was swollen, perhaps even broken.

After Keret pulled Amata out of the pit, Sam looped the rope around himself. Keret was about to pull him up when Sam saw his dagger lying on the ground.

"Wait," Sam called out. He retrieved his bronze dagger, returned it to its sheath under his robe, and then tugged on the rope.

Moments later they crawled out into the first chamber. Amata couldn't put any weight on her left foot, so Keret supported her as he led them through the tunnel toward the outside.

"Well, what have we here?"

Sam knew in an instant that the high-pitched voice in the darkness ahead of them belonged to Nakthor. They hadn't gotten out soon enough.

"Giving your friends a little tour of our meeting place?" Nakthor whined.

"Just let them go, Nakthor. They have nothing to do with us," Keret said.

"I don't think so," Nakthor shot back.

Sam saw shadows of men behind Nakthor. Several held torches.

"Take them all to the hidden chamber," Nakthor ordered.

Two large Egyptians pushed Sam, Amata, Balashi and Keret back through the tunnel to the middle chamber. Another man then pulled on one of the wall torches and the secret panel opened. Several clay jars stood in the middle of the hidden room.

"Tie them up over there," Nakthor said as he pointed to the back corner. Sam saw Nakthor carry a small chest to the other side of the room.

Three large men shoved Sam, Amata and Balashi towards the back. They brought out ropes and began to fasten their hands and feet.

"Please, I think my daughter's ankle is broken," Balashi said. "We won't try to escape. There's no need to tie her feet."

In the confusion, Sam managed to remove his dagger from its sheath and sit on it before one of the men bound Sam's hands behind his back, and his feet out in front of him. Fire shot through Sam's injured wrist as they tied his hands, but knowing he had freed his dagger made the pain a little easier to bear.

"Please, Nakthor," Keret said. "I'll do whatever you want. Just don't hurt my friends."

Nakthor slapped Keret's face. "Soon everyone in Egypt will do whatever I want." Nakthor sneered. "After I marry Princess Miut, it won't be long before I replace our weak Pharaoh and rid our country of all foreign pestilence."

Amata squirmed and wriggled next to Sam. He felt grateful they hadn't tied her feet.

"So *you* had Merib killed," Amata said as she moved back to lean against the wall. Sam saw her eyes grow wide. "When the truth comes out, Egypt will never bow to you. They know that a rightful Pharaoh must rule Egypt in order to maintain balance and order. And how can you, a priest, justify taking the prince's life?"

"The truth is whatever I say it is," Nakthor spit out. "Prince Merib was killed in a hunting accident. Right, Iny?

Over the past few years I've worked hard to give the priests and nomarchs a taste of power, and I'll do whatever it takes to make sure that no one stops me. With my help, Egypt will become the great power it was always meant to be."

Sam saw Iny behind Nakthor, directing the workers where to put the bags they brought in from the outside. "That's right," Iny replied. "After I bribed the scribes under my charge to alter their records of grain distributions, the nomarchs were more than happy to receive compensation for holding back some of their nomes' food allotments and to give us the extra grain. Greed is a powerful motivator."

Another group of men now entered the secret chamber carrying clay jars. Behind them came Uru.

Amata gasped. "No, not you too, Uru! Is there no good person left in Egypt?"

Uru's mouth dropped open. "Amata? What are you doing here? Barak, I . . ."

Barak's lips pressed together and he shook his head. "Not now, cousin."

Turning to the men bringing in the jars, Barak pointed to the bags on the floor. "Empty those bags of grain into our jars then seal them shut. Once I settle our account with the priest, carry the jars to the ship."

Sam nudged Keret to get his attention. He then cocked his head and sat on his knees, hoping Keret would spot his dagger. Keret gave a slight nod. He sat next to Sam on the dirt floor and picked up the dagger.

Iny instructed his workers to empty the grain from the bags into the jars. Barak mixed fresh clay and sealed the jars once they were filled.

Barak waved the back of his hand at Uru. "Just return to the ship, cousin. The men will load the jars once we're finished here."

"Barak," Uru began.

"No. Do what I say for once," Barak shouted. "No questions. Just go."

As the men argued, Keret cut the cords that bound Sam's hands.

Sam saw Amata glance over at them, then back at Uru and Barak.

"So, Uru," Amata said. "This is how you repay your Egyptian 'friends'? You steal from them to make more money for yourself?"

Uru took a step closer to Amata, but Nakthor stopped him.

"No time for sympathy, Foreigner," Nakthor said to Uru. "Leave before I change my mind and raise the price of the grain."

As Uru argued with Nakthor, Keret reached behind Sam and cut Amata's ropes. Keret then handed the knife back to Sam, who still pretended to have his hands tied behind his back.

Keret now stood and confronted Uru. "Like the priest said, get out of here, Foreigner." Keret shoved Uru backwards toward the secret panel's opening.

Uru regained his balance, lunged forward, and grabbed the neckline of Keret's tunic. "Look who's talking. You're nothing but a Canaanite slave."

In the distraction, Sam managed to cut the rope that bound his feet. Sam saw Balashi watching him.

Balashi raised his head a few times in the direction of the open panel, as if to say they should make a run for it.

Sam pressed his lips together into a thin line and shook his head from side to side, as if to say, "We're not leaving without you."

Balashi also shook his head, and then motioned toward Amata. Sam understood that Balashi wanted him to get Amata to safety.

Sam tried to draw in a breath, but the air seemed to catch in his throat.

Keret shoved Uru again, causing him to tumble into one of the clay jars. The jar toppled onto Barak.

"Hey!" Barak yelled.

Sam quickly pulled Amata to her feet and wrapped his arm around her waist. Together they limped toward the door.

Sam saw Uru look over at them. Uru then took a swing at Keret.

Sam and Amata reached the chamber's panel. Sam looked back and saw Keret punch Uru in the stomach.

"Enough!" Nakthor screamed. "Stop this at once!"

Barak and Iny's men now joined in the fight.

Sam and Amata continued to limp out of the chamber and into the middle room.

"Sam," Amata cried. "What about Father?"

"He wants me to get you to safety," Sam said. "Just go with me as fast as you can."

The smack of fists slamming into faces and groans as punches landed into stomachs followed Sam and Amata out the corridor. Sam looked back again. He saw Keret tugging at the knots of rope that fastened Balashi's feet.

Sam released Amata and nudged her forward. "Just a little further, and you'll be safe. Go."

Sam limped back toward the large chamber.

As he approached, a portion of the chamber's floor began to crack. With a whoosh and a crash, Barak and some of his men disappeared into a hole.

"Barak!" Uru shouted. Uru and some of his crew clamored to the side of the depression.

"Iny," Nakthor screamed. "You and your men take the grain and get out of here. I'll be right behind you."

Nakthor ran to the back of the room.

Sam pulled out his dagger and helped Keret free Balashi's hands and feet.

Suddenly, Amata appeared at Sam's side.

"I told you to get outside," Sam yelled.

Just as Keret and Sam helped Balashi stand, one of Iny's men grabbed Keret from behind and pulled him away. Keret threw a punch at the man, but missed. The man twisted Keret's arm and bent it back. Keret let out a howl.

The ground shook again. Balashi turned toward Nakthor.

"We must all get out of here. Now!" Balashi shouted to the priest.

"I can't leave without my treasure," Nakthor shot back.

Balashi moved to the rear corner of the room and grabbed the priest's robe. Another tremor shook the room. The floor opened near Nakthor, taking both the priest and Balashi down.

"My leg," Sam heard Nakthor whine from below. "Someone help me."

The room continued to rumble.

Keret knocked down his assailant with a kick to the stomach, and then ran over to Sam. "We've got to get out of here, now. This whole tomb's about to cave in."

"Not without Father," Sam screamed.

Sam looked down into the hole. Nakthor's leg was twisted into an unnatural position.

Balashi looked up. "Keret. Get Sam and Amata to safety. Then come back for us."

Amata leaned over the side of the pit. "We're not leaving without you, Father."

The room shook again. Rock and debris fell from the ceiling. Suddenly Balashi cried out. Sam looked down again. A boulder now pinned his father's arm to the ground.

Uru, with rope in hand, joined Keret, Amata and Sam at the edge of Balashi's hole.

Uru turned to Sam. "Get Amata out of here. Keret and I will pull Balashi and Nakthor out."

Sam looked at Keret.

Keret nodded.

Everyone else, including Barak, had already fled the room.

"No, Father!" Amata cried as Sam dragged her from the crumbling chamber.

Minutes seemed like hours as Sam and Amata waited outside the tomb. The ground continued to shake. Amata buried her head in Sam's shoulder as the two of them listened to the sound of falling rocks from within. Wisps of dust floated out of the entrance. Finally Uru and Keret emerged—alone.

SEVENTEEN

"Where's Father?" Amata screamed when Uru and Keret stumbled out of the tomb.

Uru wiped dust and sweat from his face with the back of his arm. "I dropped Keret into the hole so he could get Balashi out, but your father insisted that we pull Nakthor up first." Uru leaned over with his hands on his thighs, and took in short gasps of air.

Keret continued. "I managed to shove the boulder off Balashi's arm, and then I tied the rope around Nakthor's waist so Uru could pull him up." Keret stopped and squeezed his eyes shut for a second. "Once Nakthor reached the top, Uru dropped the rope down and, just as I fastened it around Balashi's waist, more rocks crashed in on us."

Uru rubbed his mouth and chin with his hand. "I couldn't see anything at first, there was so much dust. When the air cleared, your father was . . ."

Keret broke in. "There was nothing we could do. A boulder hit his head. He died instantly."

Uru reached out to touch Amata's shoulder.

She pulled away. "So you just left him there?" she screamed.

"More of the floor gave way and it took Nakthor down again into another recess," Uru explained. "Then debris fell from the wall and the ceiling, completely burying both your father and Nakthor. There wasn't any way we could get either of them out."

"As it was, we barely made it out ourselves," Keret added.

"I wish both of you were still in there." Amata turned and limped away.

——— • ———

After Sam got Amata home he splinted her ankle to help reduce the swelling, and then visited Qar. He told Qar about Balashi and Nakthor's deaths, and about Nakthor and Iny's treachery.

Qar told Sam not to say anything to the authorities. Iny had already reported the men's deaths as accidents, claiming they fell from a cliff somewhere west of the Nile. According to Iny's report, Nakthor asked Balashi, Iny, and several servants to accompany him to an outcropping of rocks somewhere southwest of Memphis. Supposedly, Nakthor wanted to scout out a new area where he could build his future tomb and a new temple dedicated to Ptah. All of the servants corroborated Iny's story that Balashi and Nakthor accidentally fell from a cliff so high that it made the recovery of their bodies impossible.

——— • ———

A month passed before Amata could put any weight on her ankle. Sam pleaded with her to accept Keret or Uru's offers to visit, but she refused. Amata continued to study at home with Egyptian tutors, and spent much of her free time playing the lyre.

Iny was promoted as the new Priest of Ptah, and it was rumored he would soon marry Princess Miut. Sam earned a stipend helping Qar with patients, but he and Qar were always under the watchful eye of a scribe assigned to them by Iny.

In spite of Balashi's death, Sam and Amata continued to receive a monthly allowance from the court of Babylon that covered their living expenses. Sam knew, however, that they were nearing the end of their year in Egypt. He planned to talk to Amata about it, but never found the right time. Tonight, he decided, he'd bring it up after dinner.

As Sam finished his last bite of the evening meal, Eshe came in to clear the dishes. "I'll be leaving as soon as I clean up," Eshe said.

Amata gave Eshe a faint smile. "Thank you, Eshe. As always, I appreciate your help."

Sam saw that Amata had eaten very little. She sat across from Sam and slowly stroked her cat's yellow-gray fur. Since Balashi's death, Amata carried their cat with her wherever she went. And, at least around the house, Amata also always carried Uru's alabaster jar with her. Sam could understand Bastet's comforting presence, but, since Amata still refused to see either Keret or Uru, Sam couldn't understand why she seemed so attached to Uru's gift of the alabaster jar.

Sam finally broke the silence. "Qar is coming over this evening to check your ankle. It looks like it's almost healed."

Amata looked up from petting Bastet. "There's really no reason for Qar to trouble himself. I've been walking on it for the past few days, and there's almost no pain."

"Well, it's also a chance for me to talk to Qar without one of Iny's scribes around," Sam admitted. "I think Iny's afraid we might plot against him, so he has one of his people go with us whenever Qar and I visit a patient. And one of Iny's scribes always stands next to us when we study at the House of Scrolls."

Bastet rolled over, and Amata scratched under the cat's tawny, black-striped chin. "My tutor told me today that Iny and Princess Miut plan to marry at the end of the month."

Sam nodded. "Qar told me that today too."

Amata frowned. "Sam, I'm afraid for Egypt's future. Like Nakthor, Iny and Princess Miut only care about wealth and power. They've already cut back the people's ration of grain and drink here in our nome, and in several of the other areas. What will happen when they are the king and queen of Egypt?"

Sam finally worked up his courage. "Amata, we only have two months left here in Egypt before we're expected to return to Babylon. Have you thought about what we'll do next?"

Amata stroked under Bastet's chin again. "I don't want to think about it."

"Neither do I, but we have to make plans."

Just then, a knock came to the door.

"That must be Qar," Sam said. He went to the door and found not only Qar, but also Keret and Uru waiting to come in.

Qar tucked a strand of gray hair under his black wig. "Sam, we need to talk. All of us."

Sam ushered everyone into the reception room.

Amata entered with Bastet in one hand and Uru's jar in the other. When she saw Keret and Uru, her eyes widened. "You two are not welcome here."

Qar held up a hand. "Amata, Pharaoh just died. We all need to talk."

Amata gasped, causing Bastet to jump out of her hand. "How—how did it happen?"

Sam extended his hands, palms up, inviting everyone to sit on one of the cushions laid out in a semicircle on the floor.

Everyone took a seat.

Qar looked across at Sam. "Iny forbade me to tell anyone, but Pharaoh grew ill several days ago. He had symptoms similar to those of the former Priest of Ptah before he died."

Qar then looked at Amata, Keret and finally Uru. "When the Priest of Ptah mysteriously died, Balashi and Sam told me about the antimony powder they found on the priest's nightstand. So while I ministered to Pharaoh this week, I looked for evidence of the powder."

Sam saw Amata's eyes glisten with tears. "And, did you find any?" she asked.

Qar nodded. "Yes. I found antimony powder near the water pitcher in Pharaoh's bedchamber. I believe Iny and Princess Miut plotted to kill Pharaoh to speed up their ascension to the throne of Egypt."

Sam slowly shook his head. "First the Priest of Ptah, then Prince Merib, and now Pharaoh. It looks like Nakthor, Iny and the princess have been plotting all of this for quite some time."

Amata wiped tears from her eyes. Sam then saw her lips press together. He knew that look. Her fire had returned.

"We've got to do something," Amata broke in.

Sam saw Uru staring at the alabaster jar in Amata's lap. "First, Amata," Uru said, "You've got to listen to Keret and me. We need to explain some things."

Amata's eyes lowered. "I can never forgive your betrayals—either of you."

"I'm not asking for forgiveness, I'm just asking you to listen," Uru replied.

Amata continued to look down.

"I had no idea my cousin was involved with Nakthor and Iny's scheme to steal grain from the Egyptian people."

Uru looked over at Sam, then back at Amata. "Barak's job was to get the best prices for the goods we bought in Egypt and then sold in other countries. My job was to navigate my uncle's ship and sell the products we brought to Egypt from Phoenicia and other countries."

Amata spoke as if to the floor. "Then why were you at the tomb, if you weren't a part of the scheme?"

"I went there to find my cousin. I saw men leaving the ship with empty jars. I figured they were going somewhere to meet Barak, so I followed them, and they led me to the hidden tomb."

Amata pressed the alabaster jar to her chest and looked up. "Keret, is that true?"

Keret nodded. "Uru had nothing to do with the grain theft or the tomb ransacking."

Uru looked again at the jar in Amata's hand. "Is that the jar I gave you the first day we met?"

"Yes."

Uru drew his lips into a straight line. "Barak stole that jar, along with many other treasures, from some of the Giza tombs. When Barak first showed me the jar, he said he purchased it from a poor family who needed to sell it in exchange for food, and I believed him. As it turns out, Barak gambled away his share of the profits from our last few trips, and stealing items from the tombs was his way of paying off his creditors. He didn't tell me the truth until after the cave-in. If I'd only known, maybe things could have turned out differently."

Amata looked again at Keret. "Is this true?"

Keret nodded. "As I said, Uru didn't know anything about Nakthor stealing grain from the people."

Uru sighed deeply. "Amata, I could never do anything to hurt the Egyptian people. After I found out about Barak's deal to buy stolen grain from Nakthor and pocket the profit, I fired the crew members in league with him and had my men lock up Barak in the ship's hold. When you wouldn't let me explain things to you, we sailed home and I explained everything to my uncle. I told my uncle I was finished with the trading business. When I returned to Egypt this week, I purchased Het's cloth business. Remember Het? You met him that day we bought the embroidered linen from him in the market."

Amata's eyes grew wide. She nodded yes. "I thought you said you loved the salty air and the ocean breezes. You're going to give it all up?"

Uru held Amata's gaze. "I also said I love the people who live in Egypt."

"To quote you exactly, I think you said you loved the Egyptian people."

Sam saw a corner of Uru's mouth curve up. "Both are true. And I don't want to see Egypt turn into a country like mine, where greed and power become more important than truth, kindness, and a reverence for life. I want to live here with the people I love and fight to help Egypt keep good people in power."

Qar tugged on a strand of his wig. "Bold words for one so young, Urumilki."

Amata rubbed a finger around the rim of the alabaster jar. She looked at Uru and swallowed hard before speaking. "In my grief over Father's death, I shut you out, Uru. I blamed you for not saving him. I'm sorry. I know you did everything you could. I see that now."

Sam turned to Keret. "You haven't told Amata your part in all of this, Keret."

Keret shifted his position on his cushion next to Qar and cleared his throat. "Nakthor and Princess Miut tricked me into helping them with the secret tomb, Amata. I'm so ashamed."

Sam saw Keret's face turn red as his friend lowered his head and grew quiet.

Sam looked at Amata. "Remember when you gave the concert for Pharaoh?"

Amata nodded yes. "That was during the first attempt on Merib's life."

"Yes. It was also the day the Priest of Ptah died," Sam continued. "I went back to the palace to get my medicine bag and to see if there was still any antimony powder on the priest's nightstand. As it turned out, I discovered a secret panel between the room where the priest died and Miut's bedchamber. I searched the princess's room and found traces of antimony powder in the alabaster jar that Nakthor gave Princess Miut."

Keret now looked up. "That was the alabaster jar I made for Princess Miut. The priest took it from me so he could give it to the princess. I was so stupid to think the princess really had feelings for me. Balashi tried to warn me, but I wouldn't listen."

Amata's eyebrows lowered. "Do you think Nakthor put the powder in the jar so that the princess could sneak into the Priest of Ptah's room to poison him?"

Qar broke in. "It makes sense. The Priest of Ptah often stayed in that room when he visited the palace. We all knew Nakthor was next in line for the high priest's position. We just didn't think it would happen so soon. As Priest of Ptah, Nakthor was more suited to become Princess Miut's husband than he was as a mere lector-priest."

Sam picked up the story. "Keret and the princess came into her room before I could leave, so I hid. The princess pretended to fear that she was next in an alleged assassination plot against the royal family, so she begged Keret to run away with her. She grabbed him and kissed, but Keret tried to push her away."

"Well, if we're being truthful here," Keret interrupted, "I started to put my arm around Princess Miut. Then Nakthor walked in on us. He threatened to have me killed because he caught me alone with her. I felt that I had to survive so I could protect the princess, so I agreed to do anything Nakthor asked me. He forced me to make the secret panel in the tomb where he stored the grain. I warned him about the unstable ground, but he wouldn't listen. When I realized the grain was stolen from the people for Nakthor's profit, it was too late for me to back out. Nakthor and the princess set me up from the very beginning."

By now, Bastet had returned and crawled onto Amata's lap. Amata slowly stroked her cat as she spoke. "So what will you do now, Keret?"

"I don't' really know, but every day I'm looking over my shoulder, fearing for my life. If I stay in Egypt, I don't think I'll live very long. I know too much."

Qar spoke again. "I agree with you, Keret. With Pharaoh dead, there'll be no stopping Iny and the princess."

Uru's eye's narrowed. "I wouldn't be so sure, Great Physician. The Amorite, Hittite and Hurrian people, whose ancestors migrated here a few hundred years ago, believe they should have more of a say in Egypt's government." Uru looked over at Amata and raised his eyebrows. "And don't forget the Phoenicians and Babylonians. Perhaps it's time for foreigners to speak up and take a stand."

Sam felt a twisting in his stomach. Maybe he ate dinner too fast. Or maybe he didn't like the turn the conversation had taken. "I agree with Keret," Sam finally said. "We all know what really happened at the tomb. Iny and the princess will do anything to keep us quiet. Maybe we should all leave."

Keret spoke again. "Actually, I had thought about going back to Canaan. I'd like to see where I came from. What about you, Sam?"

Sam looked at Amata. Once again, he saw fire in her eyes. He knew how much she loved the Egyptian people, and maybe even one Phoenician. Sam took a deep breath. He felt like he had fallen over a cliff and had nothing to grab on to. "I'm supposed to go back to Babylon and share what I've learned in Egypt with the court physicians, but I don't think I can. Since Balashi's death, I've lost interest in the healing arts."

Keret broke in. "Sam, you and Amata could come with me to Canaan. I could teach you the stoneworking trade. And didn't you say your uncle was a bronzeworker in Tyre? Maybe we could go to Tyre. If we find him, he could teach you how to work with bronze. Anything's possible."

Amata looked over at Sam. "Or I could stay here and move in with Eshe and her family while you two go to Tyre. I can weave and embroider cloth that Uru can sell at the market."

Qar held up a hand. "You young people certainly have a lot of energy and ideas. If we value our lives, and the lives of the people of Egypt, we know we must do something. You must all do what's right for you, and only you can decide what that is. Think about it and talk to each other over the next few days. Let's all keep our regular routines for now, then meet here again in four days to see what we've each decided."

EIGHTEEN

Amata and Eshe left early the next morning for the market at the port of Peru-Nefer. Amata saw Uru at Het's old seller's booth. Eshe excused herself to shop for food.

Amata watched as Uru pointed to numbers on a papyrus sheet and then handed it to his assistant. When he finished, he looked up.

"Amata." He smiled. "I hoped you'd come."

The two of them walked to the docks and looked out at the water lapping against the pier. Uru leaned on a railing and watched a seagull for a moment before he spoke. "Did you mean what you said last night about wanting to stay in Egypt?"

"Did you mean what you said about loving the people in Egypt?"

Uru turned to face Amata and then grasped her hands. "With all my heart. I want to live here with the people I love and fight to help Egypt keep good people in power."

Amata looked into his warm brown eyes. "So do I."

Uru squeezed her hands. "Is it too soon to ask you to marry me?"

Amata pulled away and turned toward the Delta. "Yes."

"Yes you'll marry me, or yes, it's too soon to ask?"

Amata smiled and turned back to Uru. "Yes, it's too soon to ask. Everything is changing for me right now. Sam might go to Canaan with Keret. I'm still dealing with my father's death. For now, Eshe says I'm welcome to live with her family if Sam decides to leave. I think that might be best for me. I don't feel like I'm lost anymore, but I feel like I'm still trying to figure out who I am."

Uru grasped her hands again. "I know who you are. You're the beautiful girl I fell in love with the first time I saw you thrashing around in the Nile. I figured you didn't really need rescuing, but I wanted to jump in after you anyway. I also know that you are stubborn, strong-willed, and not afraid to speak your mind, but I would jump in after you again and again if it would convince you how much I care about you. For now, however, I'll be content to stand back and wait until you figure out what you really want."

What did she really want? She wanted a place to call home. She didn't know where that was anymore. Babylon? Egypt? She had truly loved Merib, and now he was gone. Who was she without her father, without Sam, without Merib, or even Eshe, or Uru? She needed to answer those questions before she could move on with her life. And Uru said he would wait. So would she.

———————

Three days later, Sam, Amata, Uru, Keret and Qar met again to discuss the future. After sitting down in Sam and Amata's reception room, Qar began.

"I know you've all talked among yourselves regarding your options. For me, my place is here in Egypt. I don't believe Iny is aware that I know about the hidden tomb and what happened there. I will continue to monitor events in the royal house as I become aware of them, and pass that information on to Uru and anyone else who longs for honest and righteous rulers."

Keret spoke next. "I believe Fenuku would agree with my decision to go back to Canaan. I think that's why he made sure to provide for me in his will. I'd like to find out more about where I came from and see if I have any family left there."

Uru kept a steady gaze on Amata. "My place is here in Egypt with the people I love. I dedicate myself to helping the Egyptians restore righteous and just rulers once more."

Sam was afraid to ask Uru how he planned to do that. He knew that the Hyksos, peoples from different tribes originating in Canaan, had steadily grown in power over the past few decades, especially in northern Egypt. Perhaps Iny would end up controlling southern Egypt and let the Hyksos control northern Egypt.

No one spoke for a moment. Qar finally nodded his head at Sam. "Samsuluna, what have you and Amata decided?"

"I can't speak for my sister," Sam began. "She's always made up her own mind on things, so I'll let her speak for herself. I *can* tell you that she and I received news from Babylon two days ago that Hammurabi's Court welcomes us back, should we choose to go there. The Court received news of Balashi's death and immediately dispatched a courier to us. While here in Egypt, Balashi maintained correspondence with the Babylonian physicians on a regular basis, sharing what he learned. The Babylonian Court is grateful for his service, and sent us a gift to help ease any financial burdens we might have. We also received a message from our friend, Enlil. He now serves as an assistant to a caravan driver that travels from Babylon to Tyre, and we would both love to see him again."

Sam looked over at Amata and smiled. "Amata and I talked, and decided that home is where you find yourself. For the past few years, I found a home with Balashi and Amata. They gave me a sense of belonging. Balashi's unconditional love and mentoring helped me learn more about who I am. Now, however, I've decided go with Keret to Tyre. Hopefully I can locate my Uncle Zim, and possibly learn a little about the bronzeworking trade. I also plan to meet up with my friend Enlil when he brings a caravan to Tyre."

Qar now looked at Amata. "And what about you, my dear?"

Amata looked at Sam and then Uru. "I would love to see my friend Enlil again, but I believe my future lies here in Egypt. I've never lived without my father or Sam, but it's time I make my own way. I know most men don't believe it's proper for women to think like this, but my father didn't raise me that way. He always gave me the freedom to think for myself. That's one of the many things I admired about him. He always put others first. That was another great thing about him. Shortly before he died, he told Sam and me that he loved us more than life itself. Even minutes before his death, he told Keret to get Nakthor out of the tomb before they pulled him out. I want to honor his memory and live in a way that would make him proud. Right now, I think I can do that best here in Egypt."

———

Two weeks later, Amata moved in with Eshe and her family. Qar returned to his studies in the House of Scrolls and his position as Chief Physician. Uru established his cloth merchant business at the port of Peru-Nefer.

Early in the morning on the first day of the week, Amata, Uru, Qar and Eshe gathered at the pier to see Sam and Keret off.

As Sam waved goodbye to his friends, he wondered what adventures lay ahead of him in the land of Canaan— and what the future had in store for those he left behind in Egypt.

BOOKS IN THE ANCIENT ELEMENTS SERIES

Available Now:
Book One: *The Bronze Dagger*
Book Two: *The Alabaster Jar*
Available Soon:
Book Three: *The Silver Coin*

BOOKS IN THE WARSAW RISING SERIES

Available Now:
Book One: *Rising Hope*

Available Soon:
Book Two: *A Door of Hope*
Book Three: *A Banner of Hope*

www.thebronzedagger.com
www.mariesontag.com
Ancient Elements Trailer: https://youtu.be/QoXmqA1mXa8
Warsaw Rising Trailer: http://youtu.be/_AwZhJ9pGBY
"About Dr. Sontag" Trailer: https://youtu.be/NDTyYv8CEL8

THE SILVER COIN

VOL. 3 ANCIENT ELEMENTS

ONE

Peret, Season of Planting, 1777 BC—Mediterranean Sea off the coast of Egypt

Fifteen-year-old Sam fingered Balashi's silver coins. As the ship rocked beneath his sandaled feet, he eyed the ominous black clouds that gathered on the horizon. "They say it will take about seven days to reach the Phoenician city of Tyre," he told his friend, Keret. "I'll finally be able to complete my quest and reunite with my Uncle Zim."

Seventeen-year-old Keret leaned over the Phoenician ship's wicker railing to look at the dark sea churning below. Keret then observed the swift moving clouds. "It may take more than seven days to get there if a storm rolls in."

Sam slipped his coins back into the leather pouch strapped around his neck and then tucked the pouch underneath his tunic. "Well, at least I'll have a place to call home again," Sam said. "Since Balashi's death . . ." Sam's voice trailed off as he turned to study the clouds once more.

Keret drew in a deep breath of the crisp ocean air. "Samsuluna, I've heard it said that home is where your heart feels full. For the past nine years, my heart felt full in Egypt with my master, Fenuku. Now that he's dead, I hope I can find some trace of my family back in Canaan—the family I had before I was taken away as a slave. Maybe then I'll have a home again too."

Sam absentmindedly patted the pouch under his tunic. His adoptive father, Balashi, gave him the coins shortly after Sam stole them from him in Mesopotamia. Now, after more than a year of learning the healing arts from Balashi in Babylon, and another year with Balashi and his daughter in Egypt, Balashi was gone, the victim of a tomb cave-in. His adoptive sister, Amata, found a home for herself in Egypt with their former cook, Eshe, and, perhaps in the future, she'd have a home in Egypt with the merchant, Uru. That left Sam free to seek out his only living relative in Tyre. He'd certainly never go back to his abusive father in the Zagros Mountains. Sam sighed. Like Keret, he longed to find a place to call home. Maybe then he'd know who he really was and what he was supposed to do with his life. And yet, he had to admit, he enjoyed the taste of adventure he found in traveling to new lands, meeting new people and learning new things.

Suddenly, a flash of lightning and a crack of thunder broke Sam's reverie.

Keret pointed to the ships that sailed in front of them. "Sam, If we're caught in a bad storm, the larger ships in our little Phoenician trading fleet here will weather it, but this little saucer of a boat won't fare so well."

Just then, a gust of wind whipped across the waves, slapping Sam's face with a spray of salt water. The skies darkened. The sail and rigging flapped in the breeze. Sam grabbed his walking stick and limped behind Keret as the two scurried to the deck below where the other passengers soon joined them.

The thirty travelers found places to sit atop crates, between jars of goods, and next to bundles of extra sails and boat repair equipment. The small ship did not supply sleeping quarters since their route from Egypt to Canaan hugged the coast, allowing the passengers and crew to camp on the shore every night.

After spending several hours in the cramped, storm-tossed quarters, one of the passengers complained of an uneasy stomach.

"If the ship doesn't calm down soon," a young man complained, "I think I'm going to throw up."

"Well, if you do, I don't care how bad the storm is, you're going back up top," an older man said. "It smells bad enough down here with all of these sweaty bodies. We don't need you adding to the stench."

Just then the hatch opened, drenching them with a flood of rain. Two crewmen climbed down the ladder, escorting their captain between them.

Keret ran to help. "What's wrong with the captain?" he asked. Between the three of them, they managed to lower the limp-looking captain to the final rung.

"He had a slight fever this morning, but insisted on steering us through the storm," replied a sailor with a bushy brown beard. "He finally collapsed at the rudder and allowed the first mate to take over."

Keret and the crewmen laid the captain on a nearby pallet. Keret felt the captain's forehead. "He's burning up."

One of the sailors went to a storage area and brought back a cloth and a flask of water. He poured water onto the cloth and placed it on the captain's forehead.

Keret looked over at Sam. "Do you have anything in your medicine bag to help bring down the captain's fever?"

Sam's eyes narrowed as he slowly shook his head. *I no longer practice medicine,* Sam silently tried to remind Keret, *not since Balashi died.*

Keret clenched his jaw. Eying Sam's medicine bag on a shelf above Sam's head, Keret yanked it down and pawed through it. He opened one of the leather pouches and withdrew a few dried leaves. Sam used them once to help Keret recover from a fever.

Sam turned away from Keret. Since Balashi's death, Sam no longer practiced the healing arts. It reminded him too much of his beloved adoptive father. Nothing would bring Balashi back, but by refusing to practice the trade he'd learned from the man, perhaps Sam could keep the pain of his loss at bay.

While Keret prepared a tea from the leaves, the older gentleman stood and approached one of the sailors.

"Can we still see the rest of the fleet ahead of us?" he asked.

"We lost sight of them quite awhile ago," the sailor replied. "This storm bats us around like a cat with a dead mouse. We'll be lucky if we can just stay afloat."

A young woman began to cry, and the man next to her put his arm around her shoulders. Sam leaned his head back against a crate and closed his eyes.

———————

Sam didn't know he had dozed off until a loud *boom* jolted him. The crate he leaned against pushed him forward. Nearby jars teetered, and the floor shook. Sam looked over at the captain and saw his eyes flutter open.

"What was that?" Sam asked.

"I'll go up and find out," Keret replied.

Keret climbed the ladder and opened the hatch. Yelling filtered down to the compartment below. Sam couldn't make out the words, but it sounded like someone was shouting out orders.

The captain leaned on his elbow to help him sit. "The storm has stopped," he said, "but it sounds like we're being boarded by Mycenaean pirates."

Before long, five men with long hair and short beards descended the ladder. Each had a sword strapped around his waist. Like most of the Phoenician sailors, the Mycenaeans had bare chests and wore kilts.

The captain struggled to his feet and approached one of the Mycenaeans. "I am the captain of this ship," he stated. "State your business here."

The Mycenaean unsheathed his sword and placed its tip underneath the captain's chin. "You ain't the captain here any more," the short, stocky man said. "We're pirating this ship and loading all of your goods onto our vessel. If you're smart, you won't put up a fight."

The young woman cried out. "Are you going to leave us stranded out here on the Great Sea?"

The Mycenaean laughed and waved his sword in the air. "Oh, no, lady. We have other plans for you. You'll all soon be slaves of rich Mycenaeans!" The stocky man laughed again and then turned to the other four pirates with him. "Load all of this cargo onto our ship. Make these passengers help. If they give you any trouble, run 'em through with your blades."

The Alabaster Jar - Fun Facts

1. *Alabaster:* A stone used to make the alabaster jars of Egypt. This white stone (often with bands of cream or brown swirls) is also called oriental or calcite alabaster. Oriental alabaster is made from the mineral calcite, often found in limestone caverns as stalagmites. Calcite alabaster differs from gypsum alabaster. Gypsum alabaster is softer and can be scratched with a fingernail (Mosh hardness 1.5 to 2). Calcite alabaster is too hard to be scratched with a fingernail (Mosh hardness 3). Calcite alabaster will foam or fizz (effervesce) when touched with hydrochloric acid because it is a carbonate mineral. The mineral calcite is composed of the elements of calcium, carbon and oxygen. Gypsum alabaster will not foam or fizz because gypsum is not a carbonate mineral.

2. *Amata-sukkal:* A variant of the title sukkal-mash, which means a trusted advisor.

3. *Ankh:* In Egypt's hieroglyphic system of writing, the ankh symbol represents the concept of eternal life. ☥

4. *Ashur/Asur/Assur:* Chief god of the Assyrians, god of military power. This is also the name of an ancient Assyrian city on the Tigris River and the capital of the Assyrian empire. The name "Assyria" comes from the name of this god.

5. *Balashi:* From *Bal* and *Assur. Bal/Bel* and *Ba'al* are all names derived from the Akkadian word that means lord or master. In Canaan, *Ba'al* was the main god of the Canaanite pantheon of gods. Ba'al can also mean "son of *El*". To the Canaanites, *El* was viewed as the god who was the father of humanity and all creatures, similar to Egypt's god, Ptah. Assur was the chief god in the Assyrian pantheon of Mesopotamian gods.

6. *Barak:* This Phoenician name means to be blessed, or to kneel down.

7. *Calcite:* A mineral comprising the elements of calcium, carbon, and oxygen with the chemical formula of $CaCO3$. It is a carbonate mineral, meaning that this mineral contains the carbonate ion CO_3^{2-}

8. *Calcium:* An element with the symbol of Ca and the atomic number 20. Our bodies need calcium to help develop strong bones and teeth. Calcium is also found in the blood, muscles, and other tissues. Calcium carbonate is used as an antacid for "heartburn". Calcium is found in milk, cheese, yogurt, and vegetables such as kale, collards, turnip greens, Chinese cabbage, and okra.

9. *Canaanites*: The Canaanites are said to be one of seven regional ethnic divisions or nations driven out by the Israelites following the Israelites' Exodus from Egypt. The Canaanites, like the Israelites, are said to be descendants of Noah's son, Shem, and are known as Semites (Shem/Semite). The term "Semitic" refers to people who speak a similar root language. Among others, these languages included the Ugaritic, Amorite and Akkadian languages. Akkadian, (named after the city of Akkad), was the diplomatic language spoken by many peoples in the ancient Near East, much like English is spoken by people in many countries of the world today.

    The first written reference to people living in the land of Canaan is found on clay tablets known as the "Amarna letters." These cuneiform tablets were mostly written in the Akkadian language between 1388-1332 BC. Egyptians who secretly dug in the ruins of the ancient city of Amarna in 1887 AD found the tablets. Among others, the tablets include letters written from Pharaoh Amenhotep II to the Babylonian king, Kadashman-Enlil, the Assyrian king Ahur-Uballit to Pharaoh Amenhotep IV, and the Gubal king, Rib-Addi to an unidentified pharaoh.

    The land known as Canaan usually refers to the areas now known as Lebanon, Israel, Palestinian Territories, the western part of Jordan and southwestern Syria. This area is sometimes referred to as the Levant.

10. *Djed:* The Egyptian symbol that represents the idea of stability, an important Egyptian value. The symbol looks like a spine or pillar.

11. *Element:* Elements are the smallest piece into which we can split matter (except for subatomic particles). Elements are the building blocks of nature. A calcium atom only contains the element calcium. When elements combine together, such as the element of calcium combining with the element of carbon, they create a "compound". Minerals are made of compounds. The compound of calcium and carbon create the mineral calcite. The elements of copper and tin when alloyed (mixed) together in the right amounts create the alloy bronze. Stones or rocks (like alabaster) are composed of one or more minerals. You can do an Internet search for the Periodic Table of Elements to see a list of all known elements http://www.ptable.com or for fun activities: http://www.rsc.org/education/teachers/resources/jesei/minerals/students.htm.
    A. Which item(s) below represents an element?
    B. Which item(s) below represents a mineral?
    C. Which item(s) below represents a rock?
    D. Draw your own diagram illustrating the components of the alloy bronze. Bronze is an alloy of the elements of copper and tin. Copper ore (rocks that have to be heated and chemically treated to get out the needed element, such as copper) can be found is in granite and basalt rock. Tin is found in the mineral casserite, which is a compound of elements tin and oxygen. The mineral casserite can be found in igneous rock such as granite or rhyolite.

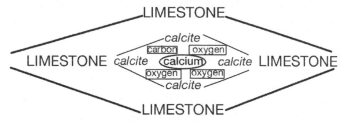

12. *Gubal:* Uru and Barak's city on the eastern coast of the Mediterranean Sea. First settled around 8,000 BC, Gubal had the reputation of being one of the oldest cities in the world, according to the Greek writer,

Philo, who lived around 64-141 AD. The Greeks later gave Gubal the name Byblos because Phoenician merchants from this city sold the papyrus they purchased in Egypt to those living in cities on the Mediterranean coast, and the Greek word for papyrus was *biblos*. Later "biblos" also came to mean "book" in Greek. Can you think of words in English that use the root word "biblos"?

13. *Hyksos:* Refers to groups of people from different racial backgrounds that took over the eastern Nile Delta area and formed their own ruling dynasty in Lower Egypt in 1650 BC. The name *Hyksos* is a combina- tion of two Egyptian words: *heqa* and *khaseshet*, meaning "rulers of foreign countries." Several Canaanite people groups first appeared in Egypt around 1800 BC, such as the Phoenicians, the Amorites, and the Hebrews.

14. *Keret:* The name of a Canaanite king. An epic poem was written about Keret called *Epic* or *Legend of Keret* around 1800-1375 BC. See http://www.jstor.org/discover/10.2307/1452252?uid=3739560&uid=2&uid=4&uid=3739256&sid=21104840757971

15. *Limestone:* A sedimentary rock composed largely of the minerals calcite and aragonite. It is mostly formed by the accumulation of organic remains such as shells or coral.

16. *Lower Egypt*: Lower Egypt includes the area from the Mediterranean Sea, including the Nile Delta, to the 30th parallel N. On a map, this is the northern or "top" part of Egypt. This seems confusing because it's called "Lower" Egypt, but looks "upper" on a map since it's in the north. It is "lower", however, because the <u>land</u> is lower. The Nile River flows from "upper", or southern Egypt where the elevation is higher, to northern, or "lower" Egypt where the elevation is lower. Once the waters of the Nile River reach Lower Egypt, they then empty into the Mediterranean Sea.

17. *Miut*: The word for "cat" in Egyptian. It is used for the name of the princess in *The Alabaster Jar*.

18. *Nome and nomarch*: For most of Egypt's history, the country was divided into 42 nomes or districts. Before Egypt was unified, these areas were autonomous (governed themselves) city-states. Under strong pharaohs, nomarchs (the head of the nomes) were appointed by the pharaoh. Under weaker pharaohs, the nomarchs often inherited their positions. The word *nome* is actually a Greek word meaning pasture, and was not used by the Egyptians for these districts. The Egyptians used the word *sepat*.

19. *Phoenicians*: The name given by the ancient Greeks to the people who lived in the area near Tyre and Gubal (Byblos). In Greek, the word *Phoinike* means dark red. The Greeks used this word to refer to the royal red and purple dyes that the Phoenicians obtained from murex shells and then used to dye cloth. The dye obtained from these sea snails, unlike other dyes used at the time, didn't easily fade. Instead, it became brighter with weathering and sunlight. Although the name *Phoenicians* wasn't used for this group of people until after the formation of the Greek civilization around 800 BC, this name is used for them in *The Alabaster Jar* because it refers to the early ancestors of those later called *Phoenicians*. During the time of Samsuluna, Uru and his people were usually referred to as *Kinahnu*, or *Canaanite* people. In the ancient Hurrian language, *Kanahnu* meant red or purple dye. It may also come from a Hebrew root word meaning "merchant".

20. *Samsuluna*: This name comes from *Shamash*, the Mesopotamian sun god and god of justice, and from *ilu*, meaning "gate", and *na*, of unknown origin, possibly referring to the moon god, Nanna.

21. *Urumilki*: Phoenician name meaning "Milki is my light". *Milki* (*Melqart*) was the chief god of the city of Tyre.

22. *Was-scepter*: *Was* is the Egyptian hieroglyphic character meaning power. The *was-scepter* symbolized power more in the divine sphere than in the earthly realm, and was usually seen in the hands of gods such as Ptah and Osiris. In the hand of Pharaoh, it represented the authority and

responsibility Pharaoh had to impart the bounty of the gods to the people under his care. The *was* scepter consisted of a straight staff (a symbol of noblemen), the head of a dog, and a forked base. In the Egyptian language, *was* not only meant having power. It also meant to be happy, or a state of "wellbeing". To the Egyptians, a well-ordered society was necessary for the happiness of the people. If there wasn't order in the society, the people's material needs would not be met, and they would not be happy.

The *was*, *djed*, and *ankh* symbols were used to show the Egyptian gods giving life, stability and power to pharaohs and their queens so these leaders could pass these qualities on to the Egyptian people. You can see pictures of these symbols grouped together on the "jewel chest of Tuyu" at http://www.touregypt.net/featurestories/picture12312002.htm and http://www.flickr.com/photos/vcorne00/4242461968/.

More teacher and student resources, including student questions and teacher answers relating to the Fun Facts, can be found at
http://www.thebronzedagger.com/teacher-pages.html
www.mariesontag.com

Made in the USA
Charleston, SC
17 October 2015